THE FAMOUS FIVE
AND THE STATELY HOMES GANG

THE FAMOUS FIVE are Julian, Dick, George (Georgina by rights), Anne and Timmy the dog.

The Five are pleased to be spending another holiday at Kirrin Cottage, the scene of many of their adventures. And this holiday proves to be as exciting as all the others, from the moment they set off on their shiny new bicycles!

Cover illustration by John Cooper

The Famous Five and the Stately Homes Gang

A new adventure of the characters created by Enid Blyton, told by Claude Voilier, translated by Anthea Bell

Illustrated by John Cooper

KNIGHT BOOKS
Hodder and Stoughton

Copyright © Librairie Hachette 1972
First published in France as *Le Marquis
Appelle Les Cinq*
English language translation copyright
© Hodder & Stoughton Ltd, 1981
Illustrations copyright © Hodder &
Stoughton Ltd, 1981

*First published in Great Britain by
Knight Books 1981*

British Library C.I.P.

Voilier, Claude
    The Famous Five and the stately homes gang.
    I. Title
    843'.9'IJ

    ISBN 0-340-26525-6

Printed and bound in Great Britain for
Hodder and Stoughton Paperbacks, a
division of Hodder and Stoughton Ltd.,
Mill Road, Dunton Green, Sevenoaks,
Kent (Editorial Office: 47 Bedford
Square, London, WC1 3DP) by
Hunt Barnard Printing Ltd.,
Aylesbury, Bucks.

CONTENTS

Chapter One

NEW BICYCLES

'Throw the ball over this way, Julian! Oh, Timmy, do stop jumping around like that. Can't you see you're getting in my way and being a nuisance?'

'How dare you speak to Timmy like that?'

And George flung herself at her cousin Dick. She was quite red with anger!

'Oh, please, you two!' cried Anne, Dick and Julian's younger sister, trying to make peace between her brother and her cousin. 'Surely you're not going to start quarrelling at the very beginning of the holidays, are you? We all know you prefer looking like a boy, George – but if you start fighting like one too your father won't be very pleased!'

'Anne's right,' said Julian cheerfully. 'Why don't we just enjoy the fine weather and being on holiday? What luck to be back at Kirrin Cottage for the hols again this year!'

George calmed down at once. She was a quick-tempered girl, but good natured, and she adored her three cousins – who felt just the same about her!

George's parents had invited Julian, Dick and Anne to spend the summer holidays with them, as they often did. Uncle Quentin was a famous scientist. He needed peace and quiet for his work, and he couldn't stand being disturbed by the sound of children playing, so George and her cousins had to make as little noise as possible.

George, whose real name was Georgina, was not afraid of anything. Her boldness was quite proverbial in the family! All the same, she did feel scared of her father when he got angry with her, and she usually kept quiet and was well-behaved at home.

With her dark hair cut very short, George looked exactly like a boy. She was lively and full of energy, and she was generally the ringleader of the Five when they had adventures. Dick was dark-haired too, and the same age as his cousin – eleven. They were very much alike. Julian was thirteen and Anne was ten. They were both fair-haired.

'Let's take the ball somewhere farther away from the house,' George suggested. 'You know how Father hates it if we disturb him while he's buried in his work. He wouldn't be a bit pleased if we broke one of his study windows with our ball!'

The children ran off, with Timmy, George's beloved dog, bounding along in front of them. The pair of them were inseparable companions!

George and her three cousins got on very well indeed together. They all had one thing in common – they loved mysteries and exciting adventures, even if Anne was inclined to feel frightened at times. They had already solved many problems which had baffled the police, and they were so pleased with their success that they had christened themselves the 'Famous Five'. The fifth was Timmy, of course!

Kirrin Cottage stood near the sea, close to Kirrin village. It was the home of George, Uncle Quentin and Aunt Fanny. The cousins were never bored staying at Kirrin. Aunt Fanny was kind, and tended to spoil the children a bit, but she did insist that they must be in punctually for mealtimes. Apart from that, however, she let them do as they wanted.

The Five really enjoyed being so free. They had so much fun in the country near Kirrin Cottage – they could go for outings, and picnics, and all sorts of things.

After they had finished their ball game, the five of them piled into George's rowing boat.

'Let's row over to Kirrin Island and have a game of hide-and-seek,' Dick suggested.

'What, in this heat?' Julian protested. 'No, if you ask me, a bathe in the little cove on the island would be a better idea. We can have a diving competition.'

'Right!' agreed George, seizing the oars.

Kirrin Island belonged to George. She was very proud of it, and wouldn't let anyone land there without her permission.

The Five had a fine time for the rest of the day, though Julian, who was very sensible and grown-up for his age, had to call George to order several times! Her vivid imagination was always suggesting new and daring ideas to her – and it must be admitted that they didn't always work. When that happened, Julian often had to step in to prevent disaster. At other times, however, 'George's brainwaves', as Dick called them, really *were* brilliant, and her cousins admired her for being able to think them up.

'Well,' said George, as they pulled the boat up on the beach near Kirrin Cottage, after they had rowed home, 'we still have a bit of time before supper. Why don't we go for a bike ride?'

Dick made a face. 'I'm sick and tired of my old bike!' he said. 'It's a real boneshaker! Almost falling to bits, and so slow and uncomfortable to ride. You remember how Uncle Quentin promised us all brand new bikes if we did well at school this term? Well, *I* haven't seen any sign of them so far!'

'We did work hard, too, all four of us!' sighed Julian.

'You can trust my father,' said George firmly. 'He may be terribly absent-minded, but he *never* forgets his promises!'

And George turned out to be right. After breakfast next day, Aunt Fanny told the children, with a smile, 'There's a surprise waiting for you out in the shed. Why don't you go and look?'

The Five ran to the little ivy-covered shed which stood at the end of the garden. George flung open the door, and their faces all lit up at once.

'Hurrah!' cried George. 'Father has kept his promise! Four beautiful, shiny new bikes to replace our old ones! Oh, look, they all have three-speed gears too! We'll be able to cycle along the roads much faster now – and it won't be nearly such hard work going up hills.'

'I think we'd better wait till lunch time to say thank you to Uncle Quentin,' Julian said. 'We don't want to disturb him at work.'

'Look at that!' exclaimed George, jumping for joy. 'There's a special basket fixed to the carrier of my bike, so that Timmy can have a ride too if he wants. Timmy, old fellow, you won't have to wear your paws out running along beside me any more!'

'Woof!' said Timmy. He seemed to understand everything George said.

'Let's try our new bikes at once,' suggested Dick. 'You've ridden a three-speed bike before,

Ju – you can tell us when to change gear until we get the hang of it!'

The children spent all morning getting used to their beautiful new bikes. At lunch time they thanked Uncle Quentin for his splendid present, and directly after the meal they set out for a ride.

'Just think how easily we'll be able to whizz around the countryside now!' said George to her cousins. 'Off we go to the wide open spaces!'

Chapter Two

VISITING THE CASTLE

The children spent most of the next two days riding their new bikes. They had never been able to go so far in a single day on their old ones!

On the morning of the third day, they met in the garden to decide where to go for their next expedition.

'Why don't we ride north for a change?' said Julian. 'There are all sorts of interesting places on that road.'

'There are interesting places on the road south too!' Dick said.

'Well, we can't ride in two directions at once!' George pointed out. 'I vote we go north, myself.'

'I'll go wherever the rest of you decide,' said Anne, who was always perfectly happy to fit in with other people's plans.

Timmy made it quite clear that he would rather

stretch his legs than ride in the basket on George's bike today.

'I can see your point, old fellow!' said Dick. 'Since we've had these fine new bikes, *we've* hardly done any walking or running ourselves!'

'And our brains aren't getting much exercise at the moment, either!' said George, pulling a face. 'Not the tiniest little mystery on the horizon! I shouldn't wonder if our grey matter didn't go rusty like our old bikes – they aren't good for anything but the scrap heap now. I wouldn't like that to happen to *us*!'

'I agree,' said Julian. 'It's ages since we had any problems to solve. It looks as if we shan't have any adventures these hols.'

'Well, let's start off on our bikes, and who knows, we may find one!' said George, mounting her bicycle. 'Come on, Timmy – you can run if you like and then have a ride when you get tired. We're planning to go a really long way today!'

The Five had cycled farther than they could go on an outing with their old bikes when they saw an old castle ahead, with a sign pointing to it telling them it was 'Open to the Public'.

'Shall we go and look over that castle?' suggested Dick.

'Oh yes, let's!' replied the others in chorus.

The children left their bikes in some bicycle stands inside the castle courtyard itself. Then they went in through the big arched doorway of the main entrance. How cool it was inside! Anne strained her eyes in the dim light.

'What is there to see here?' she whispered.

A man selling tickets inside a kind of lodge with perspex walls smiled at her.

'This castle dates from the sixteenth century,' he explained. 'Besides its architecture, and some beautiful old pieces of furniture, you can see items of interest exhibited in glass cases – pretty snuff-boxes, valuable vases, old weapons, brooches and buckles and other pieces of gold and silver jewellery which the ladies of the Castle wore when they went to court, and so on.'

Anne loved jewellery and knick-knacks, and she was delighted at the thought of seeing all these pretty things. Julian bought tickets for them all. However, just as George was about to follow her cousins on into the castle, with Timmy at her heels, the man selling tickets called her back.

'Hi, laddie!' he shouted. Like so many other people, he thought George was a boy! 'Dogs aren't allowed in. Tie him up here – you can collect him on your way out.'

George immediately bristled angrily.

'My dog is *extremely* well behaved!' she said, in a very dignified voice. 'He doesn't bark, and he never does anything naughty – and I'm quite willing to pay for him to go in. There you are!'

And with what she hoped was a lordly gesture,

she put a couple of coins down in front of the astonished ticket seller.

'Come on, Tim, what are you waiting for?' she said.

She joined her cousins, who were already gathering round a long, low show-case with a glass top.

Dick was looking disappointed.

'Are these supposed to be the valuable jewels and things?' he asked. 'Well, I must say! They're obviously all fakes – why, they're just like stage jewellery in a play!'

Julian frowned. As usual, he felt responsible for the younger children's behaviour. 'Dick, it isn't very polite to say so inside the castle,' he told his brother. 'Though I must admit you're right! None of these things can be worth any money to speak of – that man selling tickets wasn't telling us the truth. *I* can't see any precious jewellery at all.'

'Let's go a bit farther,' suggested Anne.

But the other glass cases held things which were just as obviously imitations as the jewellery in the first case.

'How odd,' said George, under her breath. 'And there's something rather strange about the empty cases under the window over there, too. Hullo,' she added, going over to them, 'just look! The locks have been forced – and the top of this one's broken.'

At the same moment another visitor looking

'The're obviously all fakes – why, they're just like stage jewellery in a play!'

'This castle was burgled only last week,' another visitor told them.

2

over the castle, like the children, turned round.

'It's hardly surprising those cases are empty,' he told George. 'This castle was burgled only last week. The story was in all the newspapers. I was wondering just what the burglars had left here in the castle museum. Well, now I know – practically nothing! They ought to warn people on their way in. I call it disgraceful making us pay the full price just to look at bare walls and empty cases. That's theft too, only in a different way!'

The man went off, muttering crossly to himself.

'Did you hear that?' George asked her cousins. 'There was a burglary here at the castle only a few days ago.'

'I hope they caught the thieves!' said Dick.

'Let's go and ask the man who sells the tickets.'

The Five went back to the ticket seller, who glared sternly at Timmy, but when the children asked him if there had really been a burglary he was quite ready to tell them all about it.

'Oh yes, it's true enough,' he said. 'We had a visit from some thieves who must have been very well informed. They broke open the cases containing the most precious jewellery and other objects in our museum. All they left were a few things which either aren't worth anything much, or would be difficult for them to sell. I have to admit they were clever. They worked fast, and they knew just what they were doing!'

'I suppose the police have caught them by now?' asked Dick, hoping that justice had been done.

'No such luck,' said the man, shaking his head. 'The thieves are still at large. And they've made the headlines again this week – I suppose you're too young to read the papers, or you'd know that two other big houses and a private museum in this part of the country have been raided too, and the police are sure it was the same gang. They certainly are cool customers!'

Julian looked rather annoyed. 'We're certainly not too young to read the papers!' he said. 'It just so happens we're on holiday, so we haven't been taking much notice of the news. But I *do* seem to remember hearing something about those burglars on the radio yesterday evening – yes, it's coming back to me now!'

'The police are hard at work at the moment, trying to track the thieves down,' said the man. 'They really had a nerve, coming here! I wonder where they'll be heard of next!'

The Five set off back to Kirrin Cottage, leaning forward into the wind as they rode along. On the way home they discussed the burglary. It had interested the children at once. When they were back at Kirrin Cottage George went to find all that week's old newspapers. Then the four children read through the papers to pick out the news reports about the burgled houses. The series of thefts seemed to be the work of an organised gang with inside knowledge of the stately homes in that area, and it looked as if they intended to make a clean sweep of the countryside. Yes, thought the children, these burglars were certainly a daring gang!

Chapter Three

A MYSTERIOUS GORSE BUSH

Next day the weather was really lovely; so warm and sunny that Aunt Fanny asked the children, 'How about taking a nice picnic out on a fine day like this? You could have lunch out of doors somewhere, and bathe in Kirrin Bay on the way back. It's well sheltered from the wind and strong currents.'

George and her cousins thought that was a grand idea. They loved eating out of doors, without any grown-ups to tell them about table manners!

They went off to the kitchen to help Aunt Fanny make sardine and cheese and tomato sandwiches, and fill thermos flasks with cool drinks of orange and lemon squash. Dick had put his little radio down on the kitchen table beside him. He had it tuned to the local radio station. Suddenly the music was interrupted.

'This is a news flash,' said an announcer's voice

on the radio. 'We have just heard that Pendleton Place, six miles from Kirrin village, was raided last night by the daring gang of thieves who have been systematically burgling the stately homes in this area over the last three weeks. Paintings by old masters hanging in the picture gallery of Pendleton Place, showing local landscapes and sea scenes, were stolen. The police say that the thieves worked as if they were very confident, taking no precautions against being disturbed or caught in the act. They left no clues behind. The police are continuing their inquiries, and say they hope that they will soon be on the track of the thieves.'

'Did you hear that?' cried George. 'The gang raiding the stately homes has struck again! At this rate, they'll soon have stolen all the treasures to be found in these parts. If *I* were in the police force I'd – I'd *do* something!'

'You might not find that so easy!' Aunt Fanny told her daughter, smiling.

George shrugged her shoulders. 'Well, you must admit that the police aren't getting anywhere, Mother! How the thieves must be laughing at them! If you ask me – '

'I'm quite sure the police know what they're doing,' Aunt Fanny interrupted. 'And I'm sure you wouldn't do any better, either! These burglars must be very clever people. The police have been keeping a watch on all the roads and ports and air-fields ever since the first theft, but they haven't found a trace of the thieves – or their haul. The valuables must be well hidden, and I expect they'll stay hidden until the hue and cry over the burglaries has died down.'

Soon afterwards, the children and Timmy were starting off down the road on their bicycles. They rode past Kirrin Bay, and after a while they came within sight of a small hill covered with green grass. Some trees and gorse bushes grew on it here and there. Dick suggested climbing part of the way up the hill to have their picnic. Once they had found a good picnic place half-way up, they happily unwrapped their sandwiches, while Timmy chased about barking wildly at butterflies and dragonflies.

'Help me to spread the cloth out, Anne!' said George. 'Julian, will you open this packet of chocolate biscuits? Oh, do watch out, Dick, you'll knock those bottles of squash over! Timmy – stop fooling about like that!'

'Yes, your Royal Highness!'

'Just as you say, ma'am!'

'At your service, my lady!'

'Woof! Woof!'

George flicked a teacloth at Dick, and aimed a mock blow at Anne. Julian pretended to be squaring up to her for a fight, and Timmy, entering into the spirit of the game, made out that he was going to leap to his young mistress's aid. The mock quarrel turned into a friendly scuffle on the grass, with everyone shouting and laughing.

What fun they were having!

When the Five had eaten their picnic, they looked at the delicious remains and sighed – what a shame they couldn't finish them all! After eating so hungrily, the children felt a little sleepy, and they lay down in the shade of the trees for a rest.

At their feet, below the slope of the grassy hill, the road they had come along was like a curving ribbon running parallel to the cliff top. They could see the sea shining in the sun beyond the cliffs. The water was almost completely flat and calm, and there wasn't a cloud in the blue sky. It was wonderfully fine weather.

Anne had eaten several of the little strawberry tarts Aunt Fanny had packed, and she was beginning to wish she hadn't had quite so many! She did feel terribly drowsy. She had to make a real effort to keep her eyes open – and in spite of her efforts, they closed for several seconds.

Suddenly she woke up, rather ashamed of herself for giving in to her drowsy feeling – though she was sure she could not have been asleep for long. Had the others noticed? They were sitting there beside her, laughing and talking. Anne sat up too. Then she let out a cry.

Julian jumped. 'What's the matter?' he asked.

'That bush over there! I've just seen it move!'

Dick roared with laughter.

'Well, fancy! *What* a surprise!' he said. 'Hear

Anne had to make a real effort to keep her eyes open.

Then Anne let out a cry!

25

that, everyone? Isn't it amazing – the wind actually made that gorse bush move when it blew!'

'But that's just the point – there isn't a breath of wind!' said Anne. 'That's what surprised me. Anyway, the bush didn't move at all as if the wind was shaking its branches. It was – as if an invisible hand was shaking it!'

George burst out laughing too. 'Well, people say *I've* got a vivid imagination, but yours runs it pretty close!' she told her cousin, patting Timmy, who was stretched out beside her. 'Did you hear her, Timmy? She was fast asleep, dreaming she was in some mysterious place where an invisible man walks about among the heather and gorse bushes – and then she gives us all a fright by shouting out like that!'

Anne protested indignantly.

'I wasn't dreaming! I *did* see the bush move – it's one of that big clump of gorse bushes over there. Oh, look! It's moving again, though not so much this time. All the same, I *wasn't* seeing things – '

Timmy's loud barking interrupted her. He had dashed over to the bushes Anne was talking about, and was racing round and round them, barking frantically. George called him to heel.

'Tim! Heel, Timmy – heel! Come here, you bad dog! What on earth is the matter with you?'

'That dog's gone completely potty!' said Dick.

'Just trying to get a bit of attention, that's all,' said Julian.

'No, I think he's picked up the scent of a wild rabbit,' George told them. 'If I felt energetic enough to move,' she added, yawning, 'I'd go and explore your clump of bushes, Anne, and I dare say I'd find a rabbit hole there!'

Anne was not convinced.

'A rabbit couldn't have shaken a big bush like that so much,' she insisted. 'It was almost as if –'

'Yes, we know, you've already told us!' Dick interrupted. 'You saw someone – only it was an invisible someone, of course! – going down the rabbit hole on his tummy. What fun it must be seeing invisible things, Anne! Have you developed second sight or something? We'd know about it if you were the seventh child of a seventh child, so *that* can't be it!'

Chapter Four

RIDDINGTON HALL

Julian got to his feet. 'That's enough of sitting about talking!' he said. 'We don't want to stay here for ever if we're going to see over Riddington Hall.'

George, Dick and Anne looked at him in surprise.

'See over where?'

'Riddington Hall! I was keeping my plan a surprise for you. I read a tourist leaflet before we started out today – and someone in the village told me the Hall is one of the few big houses in these parts which *hasn't* had a visit from that gang of burglars yet. I thought we might take a look at it before they go off with all the stuff from there too!'

'Do you really think they'll be planning to burgle it?' said Dick, his eyes bright with interest.

'What does it have that's so valuable?' asked George.

'Watches, that's what!' Looking at the bewildered expressions on the others' faces, Julian burst out laughing. 'I ought to mention that they're gold watches,' he added. 'Sir Donald Riddington, the owner of the Hall, has made this wonderful collection of priceless watches. Some of them are of great historical interest. He's very proud of his collection, and quite rightly.'

'Yes, I remember hearing about Sir Donald's watches,' said George, getting on her bicycle. 'But I don't think Riddington Hall is open to the public – and I live in these parts, so I ought to know!'

'It's only been opened quite recently,' Julian told her. 'Apparently Sir Donald lost all his money, and though he hated the thought of having his house open for people to look round, he made up his mind to do it, because he knew so many people interested in his collection would want to come and see it.'

'But if he's short of money, why doesn't he sell the gold watches?' asked Dick, puzzled. 'That would get him out of his financial difficulties!'

Julian shook his head.

'The watches are all that's left of the Riddington family fortune. I was told that the mere idea of parting with them horrified Sir Donald – he'd rather starve to death than get rid of them! Each of the watches has its own history. One of them was given to an ancestor of Sir Donald's by King James II, and – '

'You seem to know an awful lot about it, old fellow!' said Dick, laughing. 'Where on earth did you pick all that up?'

'From my leaflet and the man I met in the village of, course! Ah, here we are!'

Coming round a bend in the road, the children saw a big old stone house, with very thick walls. It had a real moat all round it, too.

'Why, it's quite a fortress!' cried George. 'You could sit out a siege in there!'

The Five cycled on, and got off their new bikes when they reached the Hall. Pushing the bikes, they crossed the bridge over the moat. There was a notice on one of the big iron gates at the end of the bridge, saying what times Riddington Hall was open.

Dick read the notice. 'Good,' he said. 'It looks as if we've come at the very best time of day. It's too early for any big crowds yet – so we'll be able to take our time seeing over the place. Come on, let's go in!'

The other children followed him. There was a gravel drive up to the Hall, ending in a paved forecourt, which looked rather neglected. Grass grew up between the broken flagstones, and the house itself seemed to be in need of repair.

'Brr!' said Anne, shivering. 'This is a sinister

sort of place. I can *quite* see why the thieves decided not to come here! *I* wouldn't like to visit this house at night, either – I should think it must be chock-full of ghosts!'

Riddington Hall, which really was rather dilapidated, didn't look as if it would be a very grand place to visit, from the outside. But once indoors, the children saw a wonderful collection of engraved gold watches shining behind the glass doors of show-cases with carved wooden frames.

'Goodness, those watches must be worth a fortune!' George exclaimed. 'And they aren't even guarded!'

'You're wrong there, young man,' said a voice behind them. 'They're very well guarded indeed – I guard them myself! I am Sir Donald Riddington.'

Julian shook hands with the owner of the Hall, and introduced himself and the others. Sir Donald, smiling, said he was sorry he had mistaken George for a boy. But George didn't mind that a bit – she smiled back at him.

'I do hope your beautiful collection is insured,' she said.

'I'm afraid not! Unfortunately I simply can't afford to insure a collection which is worth as much as this. That's why I guard the watches myself, with the help of my faithful old servant Andrews.'

Dick couldn't help saying, 'But isn't it awfully unwise to – ' Then he stopped, biting the words back. He didn't want to seem impertinent.

'Awfully unwise to do what?' asked Sir Donald.

'Well, to leave this wonderful collection of watches out on show, with only the two of you to guard them? Of course, I know you're keeping your eyes open for thieves, sir, but you and your servant can't be on guard here day and night! There must be times when you're having a meal or going for a walk or something!'

Sir Donald laughed. 'You're quite right, of course there are! No, we stay on guard during visiting hours, but the rest of the time we have nothing to worry about. My collection can look after itself!'

Sir Donald pointed to the thick walls of the house, and the moat outside the window. 'This building is a huge safe in itself,' he explained. 'It was built in the days when they made walls immensely thick and solid – it would take dynamite to blow up the walls or force the locks of the doors. And the only way out is over the moat. No, once all the doors are locked, I can sleep soundly, with nothing to fear from thieves!'

'All the same,' said Anne timidly, 'they do say that the gang of thieves going about at the moment, burgling all the stately homes, is a very clever one. I expect you've heard about it, Sir Donald?'

Sir Donald nodded.

'Yes, of course,' he said. 'But I don't think there's any danger that the burglars will raid the Hall. As I was saying, it's too difficult to get in or

3

out of the place – our friends would really be in trouble if they tried breaking in, let alone making a getaway afterwards.'

George was not convinced. 'I wouldn't be so sure if I were you,' she said.

Sir Donald started to laugh.

'Don't worry about me, my dear young lady,' he said. George made a face – she didn't like being called anyone's dear young lady! 'As it happens, I'm not just trusting to my thick walls and good strong doors. The fact is, there are burglar alarms fitted to all the doors and windows of the Hall, *and* to all the show-cases for the exhibits too. The alarms would go off the moment anyone tried interfering with them. So you need have no fear for my watches, children! Now, do let me show you round the place.'

The four cousins decided that they liked Sir Donald, and they really enjoyed looking at the watches, which were very rare and valuable. They had plenty of time to admire them. Sir Donald was very interesting and amusing when he talked about his collection, telling them exciting stories about the watches, and when the Five at last said goodbye to him, they agreed that they had really enjoyed their visit to Riddington Hall.

On the way home, the children bathed in Kirrin Bay. The water was nice and cool, and George did some daring dives from the top of a big rock.

Julian seemed rather thoughtful.

'I can't help it,' he told the others, 'but I just can't stop thinking about those watches. I'm afraid of some harm coming to them.'

'Do you think the gang of burglars might really try to steal them?' asked Dick, splashing about in the water.

'They're quite capable of it,' said Anne. 'I know I'd be worried, if I were Sir Donald.'

'Well, *he* seems very sure of himself,' said George.

Chapter Five

ANOTHER BURGLARY!

The Five slept very soundly that night, tired out after their long and interesting day. Bright sunlight woke them up in the morning. George jumped briskly out of bed and shook Anne – her cousin was very sleepy, and didn't seem to want to open her eyes.

'Come on, lazybones, get up!' said George. 'And hurry up about it – it's quite late already.'

The girls heard Dick and Julian's voices out in the garden, calling to them.

'Time to get out of bed, you two!'

'We've got some news!'

George ran to the window. 'News?' she repeated. 'What is it?'

'Come downstairs and you'll find out!'

George and Anne were soon dressed, and they hurried downstairs. Dick came to meet them, obviously very excited.

'We've just been listening to the regional news on the radio,' he told the girls, 'and what do you think the main news item of the day was?'

'The main news item of the night, you mean,' Julian corrected him.

'I can guess!' cried George excitedly. 'Riddington Hall has been burgled, and Sir Donald's gold watches have disappeared! Well, am I right?'

'Perfectly right!' said Julian, laughing at the disappointed look on Dick's face. 'However did you know? You must be telepathic or something!'

'But how did it happen?' asked Anne, sitting down to breakfast with the others.

'That's just what the police would like to know,' said Dick, helping himself to a big slice of toast and spreading plenty of home-made marmalade on it. 'The thieves were even cleverer than before! This time, no one has any idea how they managed it. It's a real mystery!'

'What do you mean?' George looked very surprised. 'They must have had to force the locks of the show-cases, or else break the glass to get at the watches.'

'Oh yes, they did that all right,' replied Dick. 'And the gold watches have certainly disappeared. But what no one can make out is how the gang got inside the Hall in the first place. It's a mystery, because the place does seem to have been quite burglar-proof.'

'How do you mean?' asked Anne, interested.

'Well – imagine the room with Sir Donald's collection in it, the way you saw it yesterday,' said Julian. 'All the windows had steel shutters over them, remember – and none of those shutters had been forced open. Besides which, the room has only two doors, and the locks of those doors hadn't been picked, *or* the doors forced open either!'

'What about the chimney?' asked George.

'Sir Donald had it blocked up twenty years ago! There hasn't been a fire in the hearth of that room for ages, and Sir Donald thought he'd block the chimney up to avoid draughts – you easily get draughts in an old house like that.'

'How queer!' said George. 'I suppose the burglar alarms on the show-cases didn't work?'

'You've guessed right yet again! No, it looks as though the gang cut the electric cables of the alarm bells.'

'So no one went into the exhibition room at all – or it *looks* as if no one went in! And the thieves didn't leave anything behind to show they'd ever been there at all – but we know they were, because the watches weren't left behind either!'

'That's right! And if you can make head or tail of it, well, good for you, George!'

The children spent the rest of that morning discussing the mystery of Riddington Hall. How on earth had the thieves managed to ransack the glass show-cases without leaving any other clue to show that they had been there? The puzzle of their latest robbery really did show how audacious this gang was!

George and her cousins felt so intrigued by the mystery that they went back to Riddington Hall that very afternoon. They didn't see Sir Donald, but Julian asked one of the plain-clothes policemen carrying out inquiries some polite questions, and the policeman confirmed what the boys had heard on the radio news. The gang of thieves which was raiding all the stately homes in that part of the country had brought off yet another amazingly successful burglary.

'What's more,' the policeman told the children, 'we've been keeping a discreet watch on this place for several days. We were on the alert all right. But as you can see, it didn't do anyone much good!'

The Five set off for home again feeling that they had got nowhere.

Chapter Six

THE SHIPWRECK

Three days later the police inquiries were still making no headway. Dick was getting sick and tired of hearing the newsreader on the radio announce that there were 'no new developments in the search for the daring gang of thieves at large in this area'.

It was all very well for George to suggest that the Five could start making inquiries of their own – the weather was so hot that the others did not welcome her idea with any enthusiasm.

'What d'you expect *we'd* find, when even the police aren't getting anywhere?' Julian had said, yawning.

The heat was certainly oppressive, so the children decided to go out in the boat that day.

'We'll row over to Kirrin Island,' said George, 'and then we'll decide what to do next.'

The children and Timmy got into George's

boat and rowed away from the shore. There was a pleasant little breeze. The sky was cloudless – except for two very black little clouds just coming up on the horizon.

Generally speaking, George knew a lot about the sea and everything to do with it. If she had taken the trouble to stop and think what the sky and the wind meant – or even to look at the barometer before they left, which would have been easier still! – she would have known they should be on their guard. But she didn't stop to think. She was just enjoying being out on the sea, where the air was a little bit cooler.

Anne was the first to realise that the sea had suddenly changed.

'Look!' she cried, pointing at the waves with their crests of foam lapping round the boat. White horses! The whole sea was the colour of ink. The wind had risen, too, and was suddenly blowing quite hard.

'My goodness, Anne's right!' Julian realised. 'Looks as if there's a storm brewing up.'

The sky was quickly covering over with clouds now.

A moment later, a strong squall of wind hit the boat. It scared even George.

'We'd better turn back,' she said. 'It's dangerous to go on in this sort of weather. There's no point in running unnecessary risks when – '

She broke off as the boat lurched again. Keeping her head, George immediately shouted, 'Dick! Anne! Lean over the other way to balance the boat! Julian, help me to row.'

George's cousins always did just as she said when they were out in the boat. They trusted her to know what to do. So there was no argument. Dick and Anne tried to balance the boat. Anne was terribly frightened, but she was a brave girl at heart and tried her best not to show it. She sat as near as she dared to the edge of the boat which was rising out of the water. With some difficulty, Julian and George managed to get the boat under control and pointing towards the shore.

Just then Dick let out a cry.

'Anne! Anne! Oh, quickly, she's fallen in!'

George rushed to help. Tossed about by the waves, the boat was swaying up and down and turning round and round – and all the time it was getting farther from Anne, who had taken an unintentional header into the waves and was now struggling frantically among the white horses. They were very wild white horses too. George cupped her hands round her mouth.

'Anne! Swim over this way and we'll come to meet you!' she shouted.

The boys had already seized the oars and were pulling away at them, trying to row in Anne's direction – but in vain. In spite of their efforts and her own, the girl was getting farther and farther away from the boat every minute. George did not hesitate. She dived into the sea herself, followed by Timmy! It was a crazy thing to do, but George was ready to take any risk, however great. At all costs she must try to save her cousin!

Dick let go of the oars and jumped to his feet.

'George, no! Wait! Come back!'

He was so worked up that he had begun waving his arms about. The boat was already unbalanced, and a particularly strong wave caught it sideways on and capsized it. Before they even realised what had happened, Julian and Dick found themselves in the water too.

Now the Five were struggling against the rough sea. It was difficult to stay afloat without getting a mouthful of water. Anne, who was not such a strong swimmer as the others, swallowed enormous gulps of salt water in spite of all her attempts to keep her mouth closed. She was getting weaker all the time.

Suddenly she saw Timmy not far away from her, and she heard her cousin's voice.

'Keep going, Anne!' George shouted.

Then Anne fainted – but good old Timmy, faithful as ever, was there! At the very moment when Anne lost consciousness, he seized her fair hair in his mouth, preventing her from sinking to the bottom. Unfortunately his hold on her wasn't a very strong one. A dog's jaws could not keep a good grip on Anne's smooth, fine hair for long, and it kept slipping out. But Timmy was a very intelligent animal, and he thought of a better idea. Letting go of the little girl's hair, he tried to grip her clothes in his mouth instead. However, Anne was only wearing a thin cardigan over her bathing suit. The material ripped, and it was in danger of tearing away from her completely. Tim was very careful not to tug at it too hard, and in that way he managed to keep the unconscious girl afloat in the water for several moments longer.

George swam up, panting for breath.

'Well done, Timmy!' she gasped. 'Just keep holding on!'

She got hold of the unconscious Anne, and started swimming towards the shore – with difficulty, because she was tired herself by now. How far away the land looked!

The two girls, one supporting the other, were soon joined by Julian. Anne came round from her faint.

'Here!' her brother told her. 'Hang on to my shoulder!'

She did as she was told. Clinging to Julian and George, she made herself as light as possible, and with so much of Anne's weight taken off her, George found she could swim faster. Timmy followed them, and Dick joined the others.

'Make straight for the shore!' he shouted into the wind. 'We must swim that way as hard as we can!'

But George did not agree.

'No!' she yelled back. 'The current's too strong – we shouldn't be able to swim against it! We must go *with* the current and approach the shore sideways on!' She added silently to herself, 'And let's just hope we make it that far! Oh, bother! The storm's really breaking now.'

Sure enough, the sea was getting very rough indeed. Lightning flashed through the sky, and there were deafening crashes of thunder. The rain had been falling for several minutes, and was simply pelting down. It was dense, warm rain, and it made a sound like hailstones falling on the water.

Though they were fit and athletic, Julian and George had to summon up all their strength to get Anne safely ashore. Dick took over from George for a while so that she could have a short rest.

Anne's teeth were chattering. She was terrified. At last the shore looked as if it were gradually coming closer.

'Well done, everyone! We're nearly there,' cried Dick.

And then, at last, they reached land.

Chapter Seven

THE CAVE

Timmy was the first to set foot – or rather paw! – on solid land again. At least, if it wasn't exactly land, he was the first to clamber up on one of the big rocks scattered at the foot of a sheer cliff. This would be a pebbly beach at low tide, but just now the beach itself was covered by the waves. So was the footpath climbing up the cliffside. The children would not be able to reach that path for at least another hour, as they soon realised when they had joined Timmy, feeling quite worn out.

'Well, we can't just stay sitting here in this wind, wet through,' said Dick, once he had got his breath back. 'We'll catch our deaths of cold!'

'But what else can we do?' asked Julian, looking glum. 'It's no good trying to get to that cliff path – the water's too deep at the foot of it.'

'Don't let's sit here freezing, anyway!' said George. 'We'd better move around a bit. Splash-

The Five went into the cave, taking
care not to slip on the wet rocks.

ing about in the breakers may warm us up!'

Anne was too tired to move yet, so she stayed on her rock to rest for a little longer, while the others made for the cliff where the water was not so deep. They spotted a cave which they could reach. And soon George, Dick and Julian found themselves at the entrance to the cave.

From a distance they had thought it was not a very large one and did not go far back into the rock. Seen close to, the cave looked very different. There was a strange green light coming from it, possibly produced by phosphorescent seaweed or lichens. The light showed up the inside of the cave and made it look rather mysterious. The children could see rock pools on the cave floor – altogether it seemed like a magical kind of place.

'Let's explore this cave!' George suggested straight away. 'It will give us something to do while we wait for low tide.'

Julian nodded. 'At least we'll have shelter from the wind and the rain in there,' he said.

Dick called his sister. 'Come on, Anne! Quick! We're going to explore the cave here!'

Anne rejoined the others, and the Five went into the cave, taking care not to slip on the wet rocks. It was still raining outside, but oddly enough it was quite warm inside the cave, and the children were glad they had ventured in.

Julian, who was always very sensible and practical, organised the expedition and set the others a good example. 'We'd better hurry up and take our wet things off,' he told them. 'We don't need to keep anything on but our bathing suits, and it may help us to avoid catching cold.'

George, Dick and Anne did as he said.

'Right!' Dick began. 'Now let's - '

But Timmy interrupted him. 'Woof! Woof!'

'Why, anyone would think Timmy had discovered something!' said George. 'Let's have a look.'

They went to the far end of the cave.

Timmy was still barking, and when George came up to him he bounded towards her, and then seemed to be showing her something just in front of her.

The other children all joined George, and they saw an opening going right on into the cliff, half hidden behind an upright spur of rock. The opening was a tall and narrow one.

'An underground passage!' said Dick, excited. 'Let's go along it! It may even bring us out into the open at the top of the cliff, and that would save us having to wait for low tide!'

'Hm,' said Julian, peering cautiously into the opening. 'We haven't got any torches to give us light.'

'That doesn't matter. There's just enough light for us to see our way,' said George. 'Come on, do let's explore this passage!'

'I don't think I want to very much,' said Anne,

shivering. 'Goodness knows what we might meet in there! The roof of the passage may cave in on top of us, we might run into – '

'Spiders and rats and robbers and ghosts and murderers and werewolves and witches!' Dick finished the sentence, imitating his sister's scared little voice. 'Honestly, Anne, how soppy can you be!'

'Dick, don't be unkind to Anne!' Julian snapped at his brother.

'Well, are you coming or aren't you?' George said impatiently.

Dick followed his cousin into the passage. Julian and Anne came after them, more slowly. The passage was wide and there was plenty of air, so it was quite easy to walk along it. But it forked after only a few yards. Then the children had to choose which way to go. On their right, one branch of the passage went farther down into the ground, and on their left the other one sloped gently uphill.

The four cousins stopped to discuss the best way to go.

'It's perfectly obvious, if you ask me,' said George. 'I mean, we want to come out at the top of the cliff, don't we? So let's take the left-hand passage, and we'll be climbing up!'

'It looks quite a bit narrower than the passage on the right,' Julian pointed out. 'It'll be more difficult to get along it.'

'But if the other one takes us right down to the

earth's core, a fat lot of good that's going to do us!'
said Dick sarcastically.

'Oh, why don't we just wait for low tide?'
suggested Anne.

'No fear!' said George. 'I'm beginning to get
the shivers – it's high time I went home for a
change of clothes. What's more, I must tell the
coastguards about our shipwreck, so that they can
rescue my poor little boat. Oh, look! You see?
Timmy feels just the same as me! He's starting
along the left-hand passage. Hi, Tim, wait for us!'

Sure enough, Timmy was off along the passage
which sloped uphill. Julian decided that it would
be sensible to trust the dog's instincts after all.

'All right,' he said. 'Let's follow Timmy!'

The Five started to go along the narrow passage
in single file. It was not such easy going as the first
part of the passage, leading from the cave. Loose
stones rolled around under their feet. Several
times, Anne let out a squeak of alarm. It was
difficult to see anything much, and the dim, green-
ish light coming from the walls was not nearly
bright enough to get rid of the shadows.

George, leading the way, suddenly stopped
because Timmy, who was just in front of her, had
stopped too. She was rather worried.

'Hullo, Tim – what's the matter, old boy?'

Timmy replied with a 'Woof!' in a special tone –
one which George understood straight away.

'Watch out!' she told her cousins, who were just

catching up with them. 'Timmy says there's danger ahead.'

Dick craned his neck. 'Well, *I* don't see anything,' he said, staring hard into the darkness.

George leaned forward. Putting out a cautious foot, she felt the ground ahead with the toe of her sandal. Then she said, 'Timmy was quite right! He stopped us just in time. There's a hole in the ground here, right in front of us. If we'd gone on walking straight along the passage we'd have fallen down it!'

'Oh, do let's go back!' begged Anne.

'Not likely! There must be some way of getting round this wretched hole – wait a minute!'

And keeping close to one of the rocky walls of the passage, George started inching her way forward, standing sideways with her back to the rock and testing the ground with her foot. She soon discovered that though the hole was in the very middle of the passage, there was plenty of room to get round the edge – and the Five did so at once, without any accidents!

After that the passage went on climbing upwards. The slope became steeper and steeper, and now the roof of the passage was so low that the Five had to bend right over and sometimes went on all fours. Timmy was the only one who felt comfortable in *that* position!

Suddenly George called out, 'Hurrah! We're coming to the end of the passage!'

Julian, Dick and Anne, too, were all exclaiming at once.

'Good! I can see daylight ahead!'

'We'll be coming out any moment now!'

'If the opening's big enough to let us out!'

Suddenly the passage grew wider. The Five found themselves emerging into a little round room hewn out of the rock. Daylight came in through a hole just above their heads! Julian only had to raise his arms and pull himself up to the hole to get out into the open air.

'Go carefully!' he warned the others. 'I've landed in the middle of a gorse bush! Ow – it hurts!'

George, Dick and Anne, in their turn, hauled themselves up out of the hole.

'Phew!' said Dick. 'It's much nicer out in the open.'

'And it's stopped raining too,' said Anne, pleased.

George didn't say anything. Frowning, she looked round her. Suddenly she asked, 'Doesn't this place remind you of anything?'

The cousins looked round in surprise. Julian was the first to realise what she meant.

'Yes, it does! We're a little way from the cliff-top – we're on that hillside where we had our picnic the other day. I remember it very well!'

'So do I,' said Anne. 'I even recognise the gorse bush – the one I saw moving. It's part of this clump of bushes hiding the hole we've just come out of!'

'That's right!' said George. All of a sudden she was quite pink with excitement. 'So you weren't seeing things after all, Anne! Or rather, you *were* – and when you saw the bush moving, it must have been because there was someone hiding in this clump. Someone who wanted to get out of the underground passage. But when he saw us so close, he had to stay hidden in his hole.'

Anne looked very surprised.

'You mean other people have used this passage before?' she asked.

Dick roared with laughter. 'What a question! You really are silly sometimes, Anne! Did you honestly think we were the first who ever went along it and came here?'

Anne shook her head. 'No, of course not,' she said. 'But there *is* one funny thing, isn't there? Why did whoever it was here the other day stay in hiding, when I called out to you and said I'd seen the bush moving?'

'Oh, Anne, do we have to explain every single thing to you?' sighed George. 'If the person in the bushes stayed hidden, it was because he didn't want to be seen!'

'And when people hide because they don't want to be seen,' Dick added gravely, 'it's usually because they have something on their consciences. *Now* are you starting to get the idea?'

Anne shuddered.

'You mean that – that this person might have been planning something bad? He might have been a thief, or –'

'Or a murderer, or a spook, or a werewolf!' Dick went on. 'Oh, for goodness' sake, Anne, *don't* start on again about all those scary things you're so afraid of! Put another record on, for a change! I've never known anyone who was such a coward, I really haven't!'

Julian interrupted to make peace between them.

'*I* think it was probably just a poacher who didn't want anyone to spot him,' he said, putting his shorts on over his bathing trunks, though they were still rather wet. 'Well, now let's get home as fast as we can. I'm not too keen on risking pneumonia any longer – so hurry up and get dressed, everyone!'

The Five all realised it was only sensible to go home to Kirrin Cottage as quickly as they could. However, that didn't stop them planning to come back and explore the mysterious underground passage again another day. They were full of curiosity about it.

Chapter Eight

DOWN THE OTHER PASSAGE

The next day started with a stroke of luck. The coastguard vessel had salvaged George's boat. The coastguards brought it back to Kirrin Cottage and returned it to its owner. George was delighted.

'Oh, I'm so glad! My poor boat! I thought it might be gone for good. Thank goodness I've got it back again. And what luck – it's hardly suffered any damage in the storm at all!'

'You'd better let it dry out,' Julian advised her. 'And then we'll repaint it if you like, since it'll be out of the water anyway.'

George happily accepted his offer. The sun had come out again, now that the fierce storm was over, so the children decided to go back to the cave that very morning – going down the underground passage the other way this time, starting from the top of the cliff. They mounted their new bikes and set off.

They rode along as fast as they could. On the way, George said, 'I really do want to find out what it's all about. If someone's been using that underground passage for something shady – well, we must try and discover just what!'

'The passage links the beach to the top of the cliff,' Dick said, 'so perhaps smugglers use it.'

'That's rather a melodramatic idea, Dick!' said Julian. 'Your imagination's running away with you!'

'Couldn't the passage just be a short cut used by the local people?' asked Anne.

'But in that case, why would whoever was in there the other day want to hide?' George pointed out. 'And don't forget there's another passage too – one going *down* instead of up! I'd love to find out where that one leads.'

The Five soon arrived at the foot of the grassy hill, wheeled their bikes part of the way up the slope and left them in a little spinney. Then they made for the big clump of prickly gorse bushes which concealed the mouth of the mysterious underground passage.

There was nothing moving. The children had all brought torches with them, because they wanted to explore the place properly. George was the first to start towards the way into the passage. She was putting out her hand to push the branches of the gorse bushes aside when she suddenly stopped dead.

Timmy stopped too and began to growl.

'Ssh!' George hissed to her cousins. 'Don't come any closer! I can hear a noise. There's someone coming!'

Julian, Dick and Anne stood perfectly still too. Their hearts were thumping hard.

What would happen now?

Who was going to come out of the underground passage?

Suddenly Timmy leaped forward! At the same moment, a large ball of fur shot out of the bushes and hared off – which wasn't surprising, because it really *was* a hare! A great big one, too! George called Timmy off at once.

'Timmy!' she shouted. 'Heel! Come back this minute! You should be ashamed of yourself, frightening that poor animal!'

Pleased to have had a little run, Timmy obediently came back, wagging his tail, while the hare disappeared into the distance.

A false alarm! Anne started to laugh rather nervously. 'I was really frightened!' she admitted.

'Well, never mind,' said George, feeling cross with herself for making such a silly mistake. 'We've wasted enough time. Got the torches, Dick? Come on, then – follow me!'

The four children and Timmy made their way

into the underground passage. Julian switched his torch on, and the other three kept theirs in reserve. They started off in single file again. This time, the light of the torch showed up the hole George would have fallen down the day before, if Timmy hadn't warned her. The ground had caved in at that spot, and as far as they could see the hole was a deep one. Dick picked up a stone and dropped it in. He counted seven quite slowly before he heard it hit the bottom.

'Gosh!' he said, whistling through his teeth. 'It must go a really long way down. This cliff seems to be simply riddled with holes!'

The children went round the edge of the hole, and quite soon they reached the place where the other underground passage branched off.

'We've come to the fork in the path!' said George triumphantly. 'There's the other passage! It looks as if it goes right down into the ground, doesn't it?'

Julian took over command of the expedition. 'Let me go first,' he said. 'I'm the eldest, so it's up to me to take the risks – if there are any!'

'*I* think this passage will come to a dead end,' muttered Anne, 'and I don't mind if it does, either! I don't like this sort of exploration much.'

'Cowardy custard!' Dick told her. 'Go on, then, Julian – shine your torch along the passage ahead of you. We'll follow.'

Julian started along the tunnel. They could see

nothing but dark shadows beyond the beam of light from the torch. There was none of the phosphorescent green light which lit the other passage up faintly.

The Five walked on in single file, feeling as if they were going right down into the depths of the earth. Anne was starting to get really scared. The atmosphere was so strange that she had difficulty breathing properly.

Even George, who usually talked a lot, was quiet. Timmy was following her, his nose close to her heels. Suddenly, making the others jump, Julian exclaimed, 'Oh, good! The passage is widening out.'

He was quite right. Until now the walls of the underground passage had been so close together that the young explorers could only squeeze through. But now the passage suddenly got wider, and they emerged into a low-roofed but quite large cave.

Anne heaved a sigh of relief – but the next moment she had another fright. Almost at once, the little girl let out a shriek of alarm.

'Oh, help! Someone's hand has just touched my hair – oh, there it is again! Julian – Dick! Help!'

There was a faint sound like wings flapping above her head. George and Dick leaped forward, while Julian shone his torch at his sister. Then George burst out laughing! In the torchlight, they saw Anne looking panic-stricken, while a harmless little bat was circling round her head. It was quite as frightened as she was.

'You silly thing, Anne! It's only a poor little bat. Do stop kicking up such a fuss!'

Anne shut her mouth, feeling rather silly. Her life wasn't in danger after all! The bat brushed past Julian's torch and then shot up to the roof. As if it had given a signal, dozens of other bats, roused from their sleep, dropped from the rocky roof of the cave and began fluttering around in a strange, silent dance.

This time Anne couldn't help screaming again, and Timmy began to bark in surprise. George scolded him and Dick shouted at the bats. What a terrible noise! But it was Julian who sorted out the confusion. He was a sensible, intelligent boy, and he had seen that the underground passage went on again, the other side of the bats' cave, so he started off along it – and as he was holding the torch which showed them the way, the other children naturally followed him. The bats calmed down at once.

As for the children, they hurried along the narrow passage. Anne, who had not quite got over her fright yet, was breathing fast. No, she really wasn't enjoying this expedition one little bit! Julian was rather worried about her. He stopped for a moment to ask, 'Are you all right, Anne? Not feeling any the worse for your fright? You don't look too good to me.'

The little girl smiled.

'I'm feeling quite all right, Ju – but – well, I'm *not* perfectly happy about this,' she admitted. 'It's all very well for Dick to make fun of me, but I do feel as though we're walking into trouble!'

'TROUBLE, *trouble*, trouble!' a hollow voice in front of her repeated.

'Oh!' screamed Anne.

'OH! *Oh*! Oh!' the voice repeated, as if mocking her.

The Five stopped dead, rooted to the spot, right on the threshold of another cave, larger than the first. They couldn't see anyone at all.

'Whatever is it?' whispered Dick.

'An echo!' said George, bursting into laughter. 'Only an echo – nothing to be afraid of. Ha, ha, ha!'

'HA! *Ha*! Ha!' said the echo, making her laughter boom around the cave in an alarming way.

Quite bewildered, Timmy looked all round him, trying to find the invisible enemy whose voice he thought he could hear. Since there was no one in sight he began to bark.

'Woof! Woof!'

And of course the echo answered him. There was such a deafening noise in the cave that even George was almost frightened.

Julian was quick to march on again, and the others followed him. Crossing the echo cave was quite a noisy business, what with Anne screaming with fright and Timmy barking – and the echo ringing in the young explorers' ears the whole time. The row was tremendous! But at last they were out of the cave on the other side, and the echoes died away.

Chapter Nine

THE UNDERGROUND RIVER

By way of a contrast to the echo cave, the Five found themselves walking along the passage again in complete silence. They were still going downhill. Julian was slightly uneasy.

'I wonder where this is leading us?' he said. 'I'm not sure it wouldn't be a good idea to turn round and go back again.'

'Oh no!' George protested. 'Hullo – what's that funny roaring sound? Can you hear it? It sounds like – ' She stopped, interrupting herself, and then cried, 'Oh, look!'

George had taken over the lead from Julian when they left the echo cave, and so she was the first to make a fascinating discovery. For the third time the passage widened and the children emerged into a cave – a really huge one this time. And before their startled eyes ran an underground river! It flowed fast between its rocky banks, one of them forming a kind of landing stage.

'Gosh!' said Julian.

'I say!' exclaimed Dick. 'Doesn't it look dramatic? Like something out of a film!'

'Oh, do let's explore!' cried George.

The children hurried on into the cave. Its arched roof was high, and there was plenty of room for them to move about. Anne was breathing more easily now. She felt better!

All the children stood staring at the river.

'You know,' said Julian, thinking out loud, 'it looks as if this river is making straight for the sea.'

'Well, of course it is!' said George. 'That's what rivers usually do! If we jumped into the water here, we'd come out in the creek where we landed after being shipwrecked.'

'We might *not* come out,' said Dick. 'The roof may suddenly come low down. If it does, we'd be drowned before we ever got out into the open.'

'Look here, couldn't we talk about something a bit more cheerful?' protested Anne.

George did not reply. She seemed to be rooted to the spot, staring at the ground. At last she said quietly, 'Look at that! An iron ring!'

She was quite right. There *was* an iron ring, sunk into the rock of the river bank and almost level with the water.

'It looks brand new, too!' said Dick. 'That proves that someone's been mooring a boat here quite recently.'

'Just what I was thinking myself.'

'Quick! We must look for more clues!'

George had switched her own torch on, and she was already swinging its beam from right to left, searching the cave. Suddenly she gave a shout of triumph. She had just found a wooden chest, well hidden in a hollow in the ground behind a jutting rock.

Her cousins gathered round and helped her drag the chest out of its hiding place.

'Let's see what's in it,' said Julian, raising the lid.

George, Dick and Anne leaned over to look.

There were three big bags inside the chest! Full of curiosity, the children craned farther forward. What could be in those bags? Did they have the right to open them? George settled the question.

'We're not on anyone's private property – and I suspect there's something shady behind all this. So let's see what's in the bags, Julian!'

Julian always carried a useful scout knife on him. He hesitated for a moment, and then took it out and cut the cord tying up one of the bags. He tipped the contents out on the ground. And then the four children stood there open-mouthed, so surprised they couldn't say a word.

A whole heap of gold coins, precious stones, jewellery and old medals had rolled out at their feet!

Suddenly George gave a shout of triumph.

A whole heap of gold coins, precious stones, jewellery and old medals had just rolled out at their feet!

'Treasure!' stammered Anne in amazement.

'It certainly looks like it,' said Julian.

'I should just about think it is treasure!' cried Dick. 'Why, there must be thousands and thousands of pounds' worth there – I'm sure there is!'

In silence, George bent down to pick up a magnificent rose made of gold, with delicately engraved petals. There were little diamonds set on them to look like dewdrops, and the leaves were made of splendid emeralds with gold veins.

Anne gasped with admiration. 'But – why –' she stammered, 'why, this is the famous gold rose they were talking about on the radio! The one that was stolen from the first of the stately homes to be burgled, over a fortnight ago!'

'You're right!' said Julian, taking the jewel from George to examine it himself. 'Which shows that at this very moment we're –'

'Right in the robbers' den!' said George. 'This must be the gang's headquarters!'

Anne gave a little scream. Things were happening much too fast for her liking!

Dick calmly emptied out the other two bags. One contained some rolls of canvas. They were not very large, but at first glance Julian and George saw that they were valuable paintings by old masters – and photographs of these very paintings had been in the newspapers after the burglary at Pendleton Place!

'There's no doubt about it,' said Julian, gazing at one of the pictures.

'No,' George agreed. 'We really hit the bull's eye when we came down here. It's like finding the cave where the Forty Thieves stored their treasure!'

Anne had pulled herself together a bit. She was such a neat, tidy little girl that she couldn't help saying, 'Those burglars must be real vandals! They've rolled up the canvases the wrong way round, with the pictures on the outside!'

Julian smiled. 'But that's just what you're supposed to do, Anne! You have to, if you aren't going to ruin the paintings!'

Dick shook the last bag upside down – and out fell a pile of magnificent gold watches which rolled away in all directions.

'Good gracious me!' cried George. 'Why, those are the watches from Riddington Hall – the ones we saw when we visited it! Sir Donald was so proud of them. How glad he'll be that we've found his property!'

'I suppose,' said Julian slowly, 'the burglars are using this cave as a kind of store-room. This is where they're keeping their haul while they wait for a chance to dispose of it abroad – after they've taken the jewels out of their settings and camouflaged the pictures to look like something else. They may even be going to melt down the gold watches!'

'In fact, we've solved the mystery just in time!' George added. 'A little longer, and all the things the thieves stole from the stately homes would have disappeared for ever. I think we can congratulate ourselves, don't you?'

Anne had turned rather pale.

'*I* think we can congratulate ourselves on having turned up in the robbers' den when they didn't happen to be there!' she said. 'Let's hurry up and go away!'

'Don't be silly!' said Dick. 'The first thing to do is put all this stuff back into the bags, put the bags inside the chest, and get the chest back to its hiding place, so there's no sign that we've been here.'

'You're right,' Julian agreed. 'We can't take away all the thieves' loot – there must be more of it somewhere, too, perhaps hidden in other chests like this one.'

'Yes,' said George. 'Let's put everything back where it was and then go and tell the police. That's the most sensible thing to do!'

They all hurried to drag the chest back to the place where they had found it. No, they certainly didn't want to put the thieves on their guard before the police had come to take the stolen valuables into custody and set a trap for the burglars themselves!

Once they were sure thay had left no trace of their presence in the cave behind them, George and her cousins turned to start back the way they had come.

'Well, we can really say our expedition has been successful!' said George, pleased. 'You have to admit we've been lucky! We'd hardly started making any inquiries about the burglaries, and we were working in the dark too – and here we are already. The police weren't getting anywhere, but thanks to us the gang will soon be behind bars. Good for the Famous Five, I say!'

A growl from Timmy stopped her short.

Chapter Ten

THE GANG

The children had earlier switched on all four torches and put them down on the ground or wedged them into cracks in the rock, so as to get everything back in its place as quickly as possible. The torches had given them quite a bright light to work by.

'Quick, we'd better put out the torches, just in case,' said George. 'Timmy never growls unless there's some reason.'

Julian, Dick and Anne did as she said. In the dim light, George put a soothing hand on her dog's neck. She could feel his hair standing on end.

'Ssh, Timmy! Don't make any noise!'

The intelligent animal understood her, and kept quiet. But he was on the alert, his head turned towards the water of the underground river running downstream. The four children looked that way too, straining their eyes as they tried to peer through the darkness. They could just make out the shapes of the rocks around them.

Timmy had not moved! He was still looking in the same direction. Holding their breath, the four children listened hard.

At first they could not hear anything. Then George caught a faint splashing sound.

'I can hear oars!' she whispered.

Who could be rowing along in the dark like that?

'The thieves, of course,' Anne told herself, answering the question in all their minds. She put her hand over her mouth. It took her all her courage not to cry out, she was so frightened!

Julian guessed that his little sister was terrified, and silently he put his arm round her shoulders. He could feel her trembling with fright, and he was ready to defend her if necessary. All of a sudden a faint flicker of light appeared on the surface of the water downstream.

As soon as George saw the light she acted. 'We must hide!' she whispered urgently. 'We don't want them to find us here!'

As she spoke, she was silently making for a big spur of rock. It was big enough for them all to hide behind it. Timmy went with her, and Dick followed them. Anne went through one of the worst moments of her life. She was so terrified she simply couldn't move, and seeing what a state she was in, Julian took her arm and pulled her away.

'Come on!' he told her under his breath.

Anne did not resist. She let him lead her to the hiding place. Hidden in the shadows behind the rock, the Five cautiously peered out, straining their eyes to see all they could.

The light was getting better all the time – and suddenly a boat appeared round the bend of the river, with a big headlight fastened to its bows. There were three very disreputable-looking men in the boat. The one who was rowing was tall and fair-haired. The other two were dark and thin, and one of them had a short beard.

A murmur of voices reached the children, who were all thinking the same thing. 'These men seem very sure of themselves,' they thought, 'so they must know this place well. Yes, there's no doubt about it – these must be the men who have been burgling all the stately homes, and they're just laughing at the efforts of the police to catch them!'

For once, even George didn't feel too happy about the situation they were in – and as for poor Anne, the less said the better!

The boat came closer, and soon drew up beside the river bank. The big fair man shipped his oars and jumped ashore. Then he pulled the boat in. Taking his time, he tied it up to the big iron ring.

Meanwhile, his companions were unloading a sack. It seemed to be very heavy.

'Here, Eric!' grumbled one of them, speaking

'We must hide!' George whispered as soon as she saw the light.

The big fair man's companions were unloading a sack. It seemed to be very heavy.

to the big fair man. 'Hurry up and lend us a hand, can't you? If it's not too tiring for you, that is!'

The fair-haired man called Eric smiled, showing a lot of white teeth in a big smile. 'And just where would you two little runts be without me, I wonder?' he asked.

'Doing very well!' snapped one of the dark men. 'You may be the brawn of this outfit, but we're the brains, eh, Manuel?'

'You bet we are, Joe!' said his companion.

'Well, don't let's argue,' said Eric. 'It's good to see our takings piling up like this!'

'Just one or two more stately homes left in this neighbourhood – and we should get good pickings from them,' said Joe, sounding satisfied. 'Then we'll be off out of the country!'

'Yes – so let's get last night's haul safely stowed away!'

The children were terrified of being discovered. If the criminals came their way, they really would be in trouble! Judging by the sinister appearance of the three men, they couldn't expect any mercy from this gang. Julian squeezed Anne's hand as if to try and give her strength, because he could feel her trembling. As for George, she signed to Timmy to keep still – he was getting ready to leap at the men.

The children need not have worried. Instead of coming in their direction, the thieves turned their backs on them. Carrying the big sack, they went over to the hiding place where the children had discovered the chest, went past it and dragged another chest out of hiding a little farther away. From behind their rock, George and her cousins saw them tip the sack into the chest.

They heard Joe's voice. 'Good!' he said. 'That last job'll bring in even more than the others. There'll be plenty for all of us when we come to divide out the loot!'

'And well earned too,' said Manuel.

Eric started to laugh. 'I can't help laughing when I think of all those coppers chasing about trying to pull us in – we're too clever to get caught. They're nowhere near finding out how we got into Riddington Hall, for instance! Ha, ha, ha!'

In her hiding place, George clenched her fists. She was longing to tell them out loud, 'Don't count your chickens before they're hatched! Just wait till we get out of here and you'll have quite a surprise. So enjoy gloating over your loot while there's still time, because you won't be feeling nearly so cheerful tomorrow!'

Julian was too sensible to feel tempted to give the gang a piece of his mind – he was just hoping the burglars wouldn't realise the Five were any-where near them. Dick and Anne, too, were crossing their fingers and hoping the men would leave again in their boat as soon as they had fin-ished their work here. They were anxiously watch-ing every move the gang made. And sure enough, after putting their haul safely away, the thieves went back to the landing stage.

'Good! They're off!' thought George.

At that moment, something brushed her ankle and darted between Timmy's paws. It was a rat!

This time George wasn't quick enough to foresee her dog's reactions and stop him in time. Forgetting that he had been told to sit perfectly still, Timmy gave way to his hunting instincts. With a huge bound, he dashed out in pursuit of the rat, barking, 'Woof! Woof! Woof!'

Of course the thieves heard him. They were about to get into their boat again, but they turned round in surprise to see Timmy chasing his rat!

'A dog!' exclaimed Eric. 'Where on earth did *he* spring from?'

'Well, blow me down!' muttered Joe, unable to believe his eyes.

'Catch him!' said Manuel, making for Timmy.

But the dog didn't wait to be caught – his rat had just darted into the tunnel the children had come along, and Timmy didn't intend to let it get away! Taking no notice of the thieves, who were running after him, shouting and waving their arms, he disappeared along the underground passage too. The children could hear the sound of his barking.

Chapter Eleven

ESCAPE!

The strange hunt dashed off, with the rat in front. Then came Timmy, then Eric, whose long legs carried him very fast, and Joe and Manuel followed a little way behind. Suddenly the four children in their hiding place heard a tremendous noise in the distance. They exchanged glances of alarm.

'They've reached the echo cave, that's what it is!' said Dick in a whisper. 'That must be why the shouts and Timmy's barking sound so loud.'

'Oh, how dreadful!' stammered Anne, almost in tears. She was badly upset.

Julian came to a quick decision.

'We can't just hang about here doing nothing,' he said. 'Those men will be back in a moment, and then they'll start looking for us.'

'But they don't know we're here!' murmured Anne, choking back a sob.

'Oh, don't be so silly!' said Dick impatiently. 'Surely you can see that the men will soon realise Timmy didn't come down here on his own? They chased him on the spur of the moment, but they'll soon realise that there must be someone else down here.'

'Timmy won't let them catch him,' said George. 'He'll lead them a real chase.'

'Whether they catch him or not they'll come back here to ferret around. They'll search the whole place, and when they find us they'll – '

'That'll do,' said Julian, cutting him short. 'We'd better start off straight away – come on!'

He took Anne's arm and made her follow him Dick came out of the hiding place behind the rock too, followed more slowly by George. He went up to his brother.

'Ju, don't you realise we can't go back the same way we came?' he said. 'The men are somewhere along that passage, and they'll cut us off.'

'That's exactly why I *don't* intend to go along the passage,' said Julian calmly. 'I have another idea. Follow me!'

Julian's idea was both simple and ingenious. He explained it to Dick, George and Anne.

'I was thinking along these lines,' he said. 'Since Eric and his accomplices came here by boat, it must be possible to get along the river and out to sea. All things considered, that's the only way *we* can get out, since we can't go along the underground passage. And as for our means of transport down the river – here it is! The gang's boat! They've been kind enough to leave it here for us to use ourselves. They didn't *mean* to let us have it, but we'd be silly not to take advantage of their kindness!'

Dick hurried after Julian. He had absolute faith in his brother. Julian's idea seemed a good one. It was a pity that things had gone wrong just when everything had seemed to be working so well. If only they could have got away and reached the police before the men had come back!

Still leading Anne, Julian stopped on the landing stage. He pointed to the boat and told the others, 'Quick, jump in! It's our only chance of getting away safely! The current of the river will soon carry us down to the sea – and, at the same time, we'll be taking the gang's only means of transport. If we're lucky, we may be able to warn the police and get back here before the criminals have had time to move all their loot. It'll take them several journeys along the tunnel and back to get it out of its hiding place. And anyway, I imagine they'll be putting their own safety first. So let's hurry!'

Dick did not hesitate for a moment. He jumped into the boat. It was a good, solid little craft, lying well balanced in the water, and it hardly rocked at all as he got in. Julian gave Anne a gentle push.

'Jump, Anne! Catch her, Dick!'

And Anne jumped into the boat too. Julian turned to George, who was standing perfectly still a little way off. He was surprised to see her looking so sullen and almost hostile – his cousin was usually such an active, live-wire of a girl!

'Come on, George!' he said. 'Trying to make your mind up? We haven't got much time, you know! Come on, jump in and hurry up about it!'

George didn't budge. 'You three go,' she said, looking obstinate. 'I'm staying here.'

The others stared at her in astonishment.

'You're mad!' said Dick. 'What's come over you all of a sudden? Do you *want* those men to catch you, or what?'

'I don't want to go without Timmy, that's all. If *you* can bring yourselves to leave the poor thing with those brutes – well, I can't!'

'You needn't worry about old Tim!' said Julian. 'He won't let them catch him. You said so yourself. He'll probably shoot straight out of the other end of the passage and make for Kirrin Cottage!'

'That's what you think! He won't – he'll come back here to look for me! And if I go with you he won't find anyone here. I'll never abandon Timmy.'

'But – but if you stay here you may be risking your life!' Anne pleaded with her cousin, terrified.

'What does that matter? Timmy would never run off without *me*! It would be disloyal of me to leave *him*!'

'Look here, George, your feelings do you credit and all that,' said Julian drily. 'But there's no time to stand here arguing! You've *got* to do as I say.' And seizing his cousin's shoulders, he repeated, 'Go on, jump into that boat.'

Since George resisted, he decided he would have to use force. Picking her up round the waist, he almost threw her into the boat.

'Catch her, Dick!' he called.

George struggled, but with Anne's help Dick clung on to her and stopped her climbing out of the boat again. Julian hastily cast off and jumped into the boat himself.

It was high time, too! The boat moved away, and it was just beginning to get up speed, carried by the fast current, when Eric, Joe and Manuel, arguing in loud voices, emerged from the underground passage.

Joe spotted the children first. He yelled, at the top of his voice, 'Look at that! So I was right! That dog wasn't on his own.'

'Kids!' Manuel exclaimed. 'It's a bunch of kids!'

Eric's big chest swelled as he took a deep breath, cupped his hands round his mouth and shouted, in a voice like thunder, 'Hi – you there! Come back! And hurry up about it!'

'No thanks!' Dick shouted back. 'We'd only come back if we felt like it – and as it happens we *don't* feel like it, so there!'

'Oh, keep your mouth shut and row, Dick!' Julian told him.

George, who was very pale, did not say a word. As for Anne, she was frightened out of her wits. She couldn't stop her teeth chattering.

'Bring our boat back and we won't hurt you!' Eric called. But the boat and the children were already disappearing from sight!

Dick began to laugh. 'They thought themselves so clever, but they couldn't do anything to stop us!' he said. 'That was a really good trick we played on them – ha, ha, ha!'

Julian had taken the tiller and left Dick to do the rowing. He steered the boat expertly along, taking advantage of the swift current. He didn't join in his brother's roars of laughter – he was thoughtful and frowning.

'You don't look very happy, Ju!' said Dick, amused.

'I've got more sense than you have, old chap. Honestly, you're acting like a little boy who's just played a practical joke on someone, without thinking what may come of it!'

'Well, if you ask me, we've got ourselves out of a nasty hole very neatly.'

'Yes, of course, that's the main thing! But it doesn't alter the fact that those criminals have seen us. Now they'll know that *we* know where they're hiding out, and you can bet they'll be off as fast as they can.'

'Listen, I thought of that myself, Ju. But then I thought, after all, the men don't know that we've found the stolen valuables, so why should they suspect we know they're up to no good? I should think they'll just take us for children who aren't very scrupulous about borrowing other people's property – they'll work out that we were having fun exploring this system of underground caves and passages, and we happened to find their boat and pinch it.'

'I don't know – criminals aren't usually very trusting folk! I'd be rather surprised if they don't guess the truth and realise that they must have been overheard. They'll be in a hurry to move their loot and then disappear. All we can do is hope that we can act faster!'

Dick had stopped laughing, seeing that things were more serious than he had realised. George did not say anything. She was sitting quite still on her seat in the boat.

Anne gently put a hand on her cousin's. 'Oh, George,' she said timidly, 'you do look angry!'

'I *am* angry!' said George, shaking Anne's hand off roughly. 'My goodness, I don't think you have any decent feelings, any of you! Cowards, that's what you are! Are we the Famous *Five* or aren't we? I'd have thought every single one of us would be loyal to all the rest. I call it sheer treachery, deserting poor Timmy. And I shall never, never forgive you for dragging me away by force!'

Julian frowned. 'Oh, George, don't make such a fuss about it,' he said. 'After all, our lives matter more than Timmy – and what's more, he isn't in any danger!'

'How do you know?' asked George furiously. 'Those horrible men may quite well have killed him by now!'

'Take it easy, George,' said Dick, trying to calm her down. 'I'm sure they won't even have caught him.'

'George, I do think Dick is right,' Anne agreed. 'Didn't you notice that the men were on their own when they came out of the underground passage?'

George was still scowling. 'What does that prove?' she said. 'If they'd killed Timmy they wouldn't have bothered to bring him back to the cave. And what good could he have done them alive?'

'But what good would it have done them to kill him?' argued sensible Anne. 'Do listen, George – I'm convinced Timmy must have been able to look after himself perfectly well. He's so clever!'

Anne's praise of Timmy did help to reassure George. Yes, he really was an unusually intelligent dog! Perhaps she shouldn't worry too much about him after all.

Chapter Twelve

A TRAP FOR THE THIEVES

With Anne to cheer her up, George perked up a bit and started to look on the bright side. As for Julian and Dick, they were still feeling cross because of the bad luck they felt they'd had, and Anne was only hoping they would reach the end of their voyage underground without running into any more problems.

Meanwhile, the boat was going along at a good pace. It was as if the river itself was in a hurry.

'I can't make it out,' muttered Dick, after a while. 'Surely the underground river shouldn't be flowing so fast, since it ought to be about level with the sea by my calculations!'

'No,' said George. 'You probably didn't notice, but though the passage we went along did go downwards at first, later on it climbed up again for quite a way. So I should think we're sloping down to the sea again now, and that explains why we're going so fast.'

'You're right, the passage did climb uphill – specially in between the bats' cave and the echo cave,' sighed Anne. 'I got quite out of breath going up the slope!'

Suddenly Julian called, in a warning voice, 'Watch out! I think I can see a patch of light ahead.'

Dick turned to look, without letting go of the oars.

'Hurrah!' he cried. 'Daylight!'

George and Anne shouted for joy too. They could all see the end of the narrow underground passage along which the river ran, standing out like a circle of light at the end of the long dark tunnel.

'We're safe!' sighed Anne, squeezing George's hand.

'I wonder where we shall come out, though?' said George, frowning. 'Because what we have to do is get back to the spot where we left our bikes, as fast as we possibly can. There's no time to lose!'

'Here we are! We're really out now!' shouted Dick.

Sure enough, the boat was floating out of the tunnel. It was high tide, and everything went perfectly smoothly. As soon as the boat was out on the open sea, it paused for just a moment and then started to drift with the tide. Dick picked up the oars and asked his brother, 'Now what, Ju? Where are we going?'

Julian looked round.

'Well, I can see the cave entrance at the foot of the cliff,' he said. 'But we can't use the cliff path leading up to the road at the minute, because it's high tide, just as it was when we were shipwrecked. Now, what shall we do?'

George was never at a loss in a crisis.

'The first thing is to get in touch with the police,' she said. 'That's urgent. And then we must make sure we know what the thieves do next, which means following them when they come out of their hiding place. So for a start, let's put Anne and Dick ashore in the little cove just beyond the cave. The rocks there look quite easy to climb. Anne, you must get to your bike as fast as you can, and then it's all up to you! Go to the police station in the nearest village, tell the policemen what's been happening, and come back here with them. And mind you tell them to hurry! Every moment counts. As for you, Dick, you'd better watch the other entrance to the underground passage – the one in the gorse bushes!'

'But what about you and Julian?' asked Dick and Anne in chorus.

'Julian can stay on watch at the cave entrance, and I'll take the boat back to the mouth of the underground river and watch that, just in case the gang decide to make their getaway by swimming out. Then we'll be sure of either being able to follow them – or if we're lucky, cornering them! Understand?'

There was no time to lose. Julian thought George's plan was a good one – and at least his young sister Anne would be safe!

Dick started rowing again, and made straight for the little cove George had mentioned. She had been quite right. It was a miniature bay, with a fine sandy beach which the tide hardly ever reached, and it was surrounded by scattered rocks which wouldn't be very difficult even for Anne to climb.

As soon as the boat had grounded Dick shipped his oars and helped Anne to jump out on to the beach. Then they both started climbing up to the road which ran along the cliff-top overhead.

George did not waste any time. She took over Dick's place in the boat, seized the oars, and set off again, making for the cave this time. Once she had reached it, she stopped to let Julian out in his turn.

'You and Dick probably have the best chance of seeing the men come out,' she said. 'So keep your eyes open, Julian!'

'You bet I will! And mind you take care, yourself.'

'You bet *I* will!'

Julian nodded, but he didn't look very happy.

The boat was floating out of the tunnel. It was high tide and everything went perfectly smoothly.

Dick and Anne both started climbing up to the road which ran along the cliff-top overhead.

'This is a heavy boat for one person to manage,' he said, 'and I don't much like the idea of leaving you on your own.'

'Well, we're all running a bit of a risk,' said George in a matter-of-fact tone, starting to row again. 'Good luck, Julian!'

And off she went, rowing like a real old salt. Watching her, Julian couldn't help admiring his cousin.

Now, thanks to George's clever imagination and quick thinking, they all had separate jobs to do, and a few minutes later they were getting down to them.

Dick and Anne, knowing how important their part in the whole operation was, scrambled up to the top of the cliff as fast as they could. They both used their hands and feet to get a good grip and clamber from rock to rock. At first the climb seemed a fairly easy one, but then the slope became steeper, and Dick had to help his sister several times. However, at last they were up.

Now there was no time to be lost!

Dick made for the clump of prickly gorse bushes and hid behind a nearby tree, so that he could keep watch on the way out of the underground passage without being seen himself.

As for Anne, she hurried to fetch her bicycle, and once she had mounted it she rode off to Dunsham, the nearest village.

'I only hope the police believe me!' she thought

as she rode along, with her hair blowing in the wind. 'And most of all, I hope we get back in time to prevent anything awful happening! Julian, Dick and George aren't nearly big and strong enough to stand up to those men, especially when they're all separated.'

Dick watched his sister until she had disappeared round the bend in the road.

'Good!' he thought. 'Now, I must keep my eye on those bushes. The only thing is, what shall I *do* if the men come out that way? I think it would be best to follow them without letting them see me. I could find out where they're going and then come back as fast as possible to tell the others. Or I could telephone the police. Or then again, I could. . .'

He was still wondering exactly what he should do when Anne arrived in Dunsham. She went straight to the police station, and told the policeman there such a convincing story that he believed her at once.

'We must act fast,' he told her. 'I want to set a nice little trap for these men!'

He rang through to the nearest town to summon more police help and then told Anne to get into his car. He loaded her bicycle on the roof, and immediately set off along the cliff-top road. He was obviously impatient to go into action. It would be a grand thing for him if he could help to capture this notorious gang of thieves and

recover the valuables they had stolen from the stately homes!

They did the drive in record time, and Dick was very relieved to see the police car arrive. He ran out of his hiding place as soon as it had stopped.

'Gosh, I'm glad to see you!' he told the policeman. 'Look – one of the ways out of the underground passage is here, in among these bushes. But I haven't seen any of the men come out of it yet.'

Just at that moment another police car screeched round the corner and came to a halt. The reinforcements had arrived just in time. The policeman explained the situation briefly.

'Right!' said the sergeant, who had just arrived, taking control. Turning to one of his men, he said, 'Okay, Fred, you take over from this young man! And blow your whistle if you see anything happening.'

'Yes, Sergeant.'

Followed by the other policemen, the sergeant started clambering down to the foot of the cliff. Dick and Anne followed him.

Julian saw them coming. 'No one's come out of this cave yet,' he told the police, just as Dick had done. 'I'm sure of that!'

Anne turned quite pale.

'Oh, my goodness!' she murmured. 'Then – then that means George must have had to face the criminals all on her own!'

Julian cupped his hands round his mouth, turned towards the sea and shouted, 'George! Come back here, George!'

In a minute George appeared, rowing back round the rocky promontory which had hidden her from view. 'Have you seen the thieves yet?' she shouted when she saw the policemen. 'No? Well, I haven't either! So that means they must still be down there in the underground caves and passages!'

'Let's go and take a look,' said the sergeant.

He would rather not have taken the four cousins too, but he and his men needed someone to guide them. Julian said he would go – and as Dick, George and Anne all insisted on accompanying him, the sergeant ended up by saying they could all four come.

'After all,' he told them, 'I doubt if there'll be any danger. The men thought they were quite safe, so it's not very likely they'll be armed.'

He left one policeman on guard outside in the boat, to watch the mouth of the underground river, and then went into the cave, along with the children and the other two police constables.

Chapter Thirteen

WHERE HAS THE GANG GONE?

They all went along the passage in silence. When they reached the place where the path forked, Julian unhesitatingly chose the passage going downwards. Before they went through the bats' cave, George advised them to put their torches out so as not to rouse the creatures clinging to the rock, and when they came to the echo cave, she said it would be a good idea to walk as quietly as possible, so that the gang wouldn't know they were coming. At last, keeping on the alert the whole time, the little party came out on the banks of the underground river.

They had not seen a sign of the thieves yet. Had they really stayed down here by the river all this time? No – to the dismay of the four children, there was no sign of them in the huge cave with the river running through it either!

The men had just disappeared in a most

mysterious way – it was like a conjuring trick. The police sergeant frowned.

'I hope you kids haven't been amusing yourselves by trying to fool us,' he said. 'Are you quite sure of what you saw?'

'Absolutely positive!' cried Julian. He gave them a rapid description of the thieves.

'And their haul's hidden just over there, too!' said Dick. 'Go and look at it!'

But there was yet another disappointment in store for the children. The chests containing the valuables had disappeared from their hiding places.

'All the same,' Dick told the policemen, 'I can swear to it that the pictures and jewellery and so on stolen from the stately homes *were* there!'

The sergeant bent down to pick something up.

'Oh yes, I believe you all right,' he said, heaving a deep sigh. 'Look – they left a gold watch behind. That's evidence, and no mistake! I'm afraid our friends have left, taking their haul with them!'

'But they can't have done!' Julian protested. 'There were three of us watching the three ways out the whole time! The men simply *must* be hiding somewhere near here!'

At that moment he was interrupted by joyous barking.

'Woof! Woof!'

George's face lit up at once. 'Timmy!' she cried.

She would have recognised her own dog's bark among a thousand.

Sure enough, it really was Timmy, racing up as if he had come out of thin air! He leaped into his little mistress's arms and licked her face enthusiastically with his big wet tongue.

George didn't have the heart to scold him for going after that rat earlier in the day – she was so pleased to see him safe and sound again! She had been afraid some harm might have come to him, and then, all the time they were going down the underground passage with the police, she had been wondering if they would find him. Now, just as she was beginning to give up hope again, here he was – her own dear old Timmy, quite beside himself with delight at being back with her.

She patted his hairy head. 'Timmy! Good old Timmy! Where *have* you been?' she asked.

The clever dog seemed to understand. Turning round at once, he made for the shadows from which he had emerged.

'Woof! Woof!'

'Let's follow him!' said George. 'I'm sure he wants to show us something.'

Julian, Dick, Anne and the policemen followed George. Suddenly she gave an exclamation of surprise. 'Look, *another* passage, one we haven't found before. Timmy was hiding there! I wonder where he's taking us? I bet this is the way the gang got out. Oh, my goodness, what bad luck we didn't know about this branch of the passage before!'

She was already starting along it when the sergeant stopped her.

'Hold on, miss! It's my job to go first, along with my men. You can never be too careful.'

And like it or not, the children had to let the policemen take the lead this time.

The way into this new passage was so narrow that it was difficult to spot it, but the passage itself was big and well ventilated. They could walk along it quite easily. They went along underground for so long that the sergeant began to get worried.

'Why, we must have come nearly a mile by now!' he said.

Suddenly the passage turned a corner – and they saw that Timmy had stopped in front of what looked like a dead end. He was standing on his back legs, with his front paws up against the rock.

'Woof! Woof!'

Spotting a ring set in the stone, the sergeant tugged it – and the rock moved on a pivot, showing them a secret staircase climbing quite steeply upwards. The policemen and the children climbed it in silence.

What would they find at the top of the stairs?

George counted twenty steps. When they reached the top, the sergeant and his men stopped.

'Seems we can't get any farther!' said the

sergeant, sounding annoyed. 'I can't see anything ahead but a smooth wall. However, there must *be* a way out somewhere, if only we can find it!'

Dick joined the sergeant.

'Can I have a go?' he asked. 'I've got an idea.'

And he ran his fingers nimbly along an almost invisible line. There was a sudden click – and a square panel swung round on another pivot, showing them a faint light beyond. The sergeant immediately pushed Dick aside.

'Let us go first,' he told the boy. 'It may be dangerous.'

Taking careful precautions, the three men slipped in through the opening. The children followed them without asking permission first.

'Why – we're in the big exhibition room in Riddington Hall!' whispered Anne.

Sure enough, the policemen and the children had come out in the room with the glass show-cases, where Sir Donald Riddington had shown the four cousins his valuable collection only a few days before. Looking round, the children saw that the entrance to the secret staircase and the underground passage they had just come along was hidden by the back wall of the huge fireplace.

After that, they could see just what had happened.

The gang had come along the secret passage to burgle the Hall, and taken Sir Donald's gold watches back with them the same way. That solved the mystery of how they had got into the Hall without tampering with the doors and windows. And only a little while ago, they must have made their escape from the underground cave the same way, taking their haul with them!

'That explains it!' said one of the policemen. 'Our birds flew this way – along with the jewels, the money, the watches and the paintings. They knew about that passage and they made use of it when they wanted a secret way out. But I wonder just how they managed it – in broad daylight, without being stopped by Sir Donald or his man Andrews, let alone the visitors to the house!'

'That's easy,' said the sergeant, looking crest-fallen. 'As it happens, the house isn't open to visitors at all today – and I can't see old Sir Donald and Andrews standing up to three desperate criminals for long.'

'Oh, gosh!' said Julian, feeling worried. 'Do you think those men may have hurt Sir Donald and his servant?'

'We'd better go and look for them,' said the sergeant, and turning to his men he added, 'Search the whole place!'

The children went with the policemen, who paused in the doorway of every room before going in to make sure there was no danger lurking there. That was just police routine, because they knew the criminals must be far away by now.

There was no one at all on the ground floor of

There were Sir Donald and his servant, tightly bound and gagged.

the Hall, but up on the first floor the policemen and the children heard faint grunting sounds. They all made for the room where the noises seemed to be coming from. It was obviously Sir Donald's bedroom. The little party stopped in the doorway, listening hard.

'Over there!' cried George, pointing to a big wardrobe.

The sergeant turned the key in the lock of the wardrobe door and opened it. There were Sir Donald and his servant, lying side by side in the huge cupboard, tightly bound and gagged.

'Sir Donald!' cried Julian. 'Quick, we must get him out of there!'

No sooner said than done, because Julian was already kneeling beside Sir Donald. He removed the gag and cut the ropes with his scout knife. Meanwhile, the sergeant was setting Andrews free.

'Have you been wounded?' he asked the two men.

'No,' said Sir Donald. 'But those villains didn't spare our feelings! All the time they were tying us up, they boasted about stealing my watches. What impudence! They actually laughed as they told us they were about to walk out through the front door, and they weren't at all worried about the police – they said they were cleverer than the police force anyway, and they didn't intend to leave this part of the country until they'd made a clean sweep of all the treasures in its stately homes!'

The sergeant was red with anger. 'Well, their boastfulness may be their undoing!' he grunted.

'Meanwhile, however,' said Sir Donald bitterly, 'the rascals are still at large – with my precious watches! And to think they aren't even insured! The money that opening the house to tourists brought in was my only means of support – I'm a ruined man now!'

Anne felt tears come to her eyes. She went over to poor old Sir Donald and gently took his hand.

'You must trust the police, Sir Donald,' she said in her gentle voice. 'And the five of us will do all we can to get your collection back, too.'

Julian smiled.

'You're taking on rather a job there, Anne. We're not quite fully fledged detectives yet!'

'But we *will* do our very best to track down the gang!' George assured Sir Donald firmly. 'Just as Anne says.'

Chapter Fourteen

GEORGE'S BRIGHT IDEA

Over the next two days, George and her cousins spent most of their time finding out how the police were getting on with their inquiries. They even went back to Riddington Hall to talk to Sir Donald again – and even more important, to talk to the policemen working on the case.

Sir Donald could not tell them anything new. Poor old man – he was terribly upset. Anne in particular, being very tender-hearted, felt really sorry for him.

They met the policeman they had seen at the Hall before, just after it was burgled, when he told them what was going on. He was rather chilly in his manner to them this time – obviously he didn't like having to admit that all his work was getting him nowhere. The Five soon left the Hall.

That afternoon, the children discussed their findings in the garden of Kirrin Cottage. It turned out that Julian, for one, was feeling rather pessimistic.

'The gang hasn't been heard of again,' he said gloomily. 'If you ask me, they've taken fright and probably left the area, in spite of their boasting to Sir Donald.'

'I'm not so sure of that,' said George. 'They could quite well be lying low for a while, before bringing off another big burglary!'

'And meanwhile we've lost track of them,' sighed Dick. 'We haven't the faintest idea where to look for Eric and Co. – not to mention all that stolen property!'

'I suppose all we can do is wait and hope for a stroke of luck,' was Anne's suggestion.

Next day the news bulletin on the local radio station seemed to prove George right. The newsreader announced that an old house called Dangerfield Abbey, about twenty miles from Kirrin, had been ransacked the previous night. This time, the audacious thieves had stolen some valuable gold and silver plate, some priceless miniatures, and jewellery worth thousands of pounds.

'There!' said George. 'That shows that Eric, Joe and Manuel are still in these parts.'

'Unless there's a rival gang at work,' Julian suggested.

'That's not likely – one gang of criminals wouldn't poach on another gang's territory, would they? No, the men who burgled Riddington Hall are doing just what they said they'd do – making a clean sweep of the treasures of all the stately homes in this part of the country. Well, we must make sure we catch them before they carry out their threat!'

'But how?' asked Dick. 'The police are on their mettle, and they've searched all the caves along the coast. *And* they've combed any rocky areas for hiding places, and investigated all the woods and wild stretches of moorland in this part of the country, and they haven't found a thing. You must admit our gang of thieves is very clever!'

Julian scratched his head.

'What I'd like to know,' he said, 'is where they've hidden their haul. They must have done it in a hurry, because they didn't have very much time. So their new hiding place can't be far from Riddington Hall.'

'What's more,' added Anne, 'they must have chosen somewhere quite large. Those chests were pretty big.'

Dick agreed. 'In fact, I should think it must be somewhere big enough for *them* to hide in, too, until the police have finished searching the countryside,' he said.

'Well, the police inquiries aren't getting anywhere,' Julian went on, 'and I can only see one explanation. If you ask me, this gang knows the lie of the land very well indeed – better than we do, *or* the police.'

'What do you think, George?' asked Anne, seeing that her cousin was obviously thinking hard, but was not saying anything.

'What do I think?' said George slowly. 'Well, the other day the thieves got to their hideout in the cave by boat. A boat is a quiet means of transport, and a common one in these parts too, with so many fishermen. It meant they could move around without being noticed more easily than in a car, for instance. Now they haven't got their boat any more – and they needed to find a hiding place big enough to take them *and* their haul. They had to find it very quickly, too. So they can only have hidden – '

'Where?' asked the other three in suspense.

'Why, back in the cave where we first came across them, of course!'

Dick looked staggered.

'You mean they could have gone back to their old den again?'

'Why not? It's the very last place where anyone would think of looking for them!'

The theory George had worked out and explained to her cousins struck them as a very bright idea. Julian was the first to recover from his surprise.

'My word, you could well be right!' he said. 'That cave really *is* the only place the police haven't thought of. As they didn't find the gang there when they first hoped to corner them, they very soon lost interest in that part of the network of underground passages.'

'If the gang really did go back to their old cave, you have to admit they're very daring criminals!' added Anne.

'They've already proved that,' Dick pointed out. 'In fact, *I* think they've got more nerve than intelligence! The police were watching the ports to make sure they didn't get out of the country – and all the time the gang was stealing more and more treasures and storing them very close to the actual houses they'd been stolen from! Everyone thought the thieves would try to get away as fast as possible, but they just went on calmly burgling more stately homes – and taking their time about it. The police put up road blocks, so they got about in that boat of theirs, rowing round the coast! Why, it really *wouldn't* be surprising if they went back to their old haunts, as George suggests. In fact, they're probably feeling quite safe there!'

George, who had been perched on a little wall, jumped down.

'Well, all we have to do is go and see!' she said calmly. 'I suggest we go back to the cave with the underground river running through it tonight.'

'You're crazy!' cried Anne, in horror. 'It'd be putting our heads into the lion's mouth!'

'Not at all! The thieves must have to go out sometimes, to get stocks of provisions. And they can't leave their hiding place except at night, under cover of dark. So we can go along the passage to their cave at night, and get the treasures out again the same way!'

'George,' said Julian very firmly, 'I entirely agree with Anne! It *would* be crazy to go back to that cave! What we ought to do is tell the police, and then if they think you're right – '

George interrupted her cousin.

'But if they think I'm wrong, we'll have lost precious time! No, Ju, that won't do! We must take action ourselves. After all, the Five have already proved they *can* take daring action on their own, and very effectively too – haven't they?'

'It really isn't very sensible,' objected Julian.

'Listen, everyone,' said Dick, 'why don't we go there, as George suggests – but leaving a note of explanation behind for your parents, George? That would be daring *and* sensible. And then, if we get into any kind of trouble, at least Uncle Quentin will know where we are. Well, what do you think?'

It took George quite a long time to persuade Julian that Dick's idea was a good one – and much less time to scribble a note for her father! The children spent the rest of the day impatiently waiting for evening, and working out their expedition in detail. They must take as few risks as possible, so they tried to think of everything.

'If you ask me, the safest way to get into the cave is upstream along the river itself,' said Dick.

'The men have lost their own boat – and George's boat is mended now. If we go that way we won't risk meeting the thieves in the passage on their way out of their den. And if we see them still inside the cave as we get near, all we have to do is turn round and go back. They won't be able to follow us!'

'No, they won't,' said Julian. 'But you're forgetting that it will take us an awfully long time to get to the cave if we go by boat! It would be much quicker to ride our bikes to the opening of the tunnel among the gorse bushes.'

'Yes,' said George. 'And if we all strap carriers and baskets to the backs and fronts of our bikes, we ought to be able to get the stolen valuables away. We'll take the biggest bicycle baskets we can find in the shed – better safe than sorry!'

'Safe?' said Julian. 'I don't see anything very *safe* about this expedition at all! Still, since we seem to have settled the details, let's start as soon as it's dark.'

'But how shall we explain to Aunt Fanny and Uncle Quentin that we want to go out on our bikes?' Anne wondered.

'Oh, we'll just say we feel like going for a little ride after supper for the good of our health! We shan't be lying, either. The fresh air *will* do us good – I feel all on edge!' said George.

It was one of George's principles that she absolutely never told lies. On the very few occasions when she really couldn't allow herself the luxury of telling the whole truth, at least she didn't say anything that was actually *un*true. When the Five set off that evening, however, she did have a rather guilty conscience. She knew they would never have gone out 'for the good of their health' if they hadn't decided to explore the cave!

Aunt Fanny did not suspect anything as she watched the children leave. She didn't even think it was odd that they all had both carriers and baskets on their bicycles, just to go for a little evening ride!

Chapter Fifteen

DISASTER STRIKES

Once they were on the road which would bring them to the gorse bushes above the underground passage, the children rode along fast, because it was some way to go. None of them talked much, and even Timmy was quiet. It was almost as if some secret threat were hovering over the four children and the dog.

It was bright moonlight when the Five reached the top of the cliff. They were very familiar with the landscape here by now!

After hiding their bicycles in the nearby spinney, they cautiously approached the big clump of bushes hiding the entrance to the underground passage. Julian stood and listened for quite a long time before he would let George, Dick and Anne follow him into the passage itself. Timmy would never leave George unless he positively had to, so of course he was sticking close to her as usual.

'Aren't we going to leave someone on guard outside?' asked Anne.

'No,' said Julian. 'I don't see what real use that would be. I think we ought to keep together. But we must be on the alert the whole time, and at the first sign of danger we must turn round straight away and come back!'

The children made their way slowly and cautiously as far as the echo cave. They all held their breath as they crossed the cave. Yes, everything was going smoothly so far! They hadn't met anyone, and to judge by the silence round them, there really *wasn't* anyone in the network of underground caves and passages.

Just before they were near the entrance to what they had christened 'the gang's cave', Julian ordered them to stop, while he went on ahead scouting. He soon came back, with a broad smile on his face.

'All clear!' he told them. 'I even took a look at the places where the chests were hidden before – and George's guess was quite right! The burglars really *have* brought their haul back to their old den. And they're not in the cave themselves at the moment either!'

The others were delighted to hear these two bits of good news, though they kept quiet about it. So

George had been right when she worked out her theory!

All they had to do now was put their plan into action!

Feeling very pleased with themselves, the Five went on again. All the children felt their hearts beating fast. This time, at last, they were really going to reap the reward of their efforts! They had found the stolen property once before, only to lose it again. However, it looked as if they were going to have another chance to retrieve it, and they certainly didn't intend to let that chance slip by. This was almost more than they could have hoped for!

George was quietly congratulating herself on their success – because she already felt sure that the expedition *would* be a success! Dick was thinking happily of the police and how impressed they would be by the courage and intelligence of the Five. They really would be the 'Famous Five' now! For once Anne forgot her own fears as she realised that victory was very close. Even Julian, usually so down-to-earth and sensible, felt they had as good as done what they set out to do already.

Perhaps Timmy was the only one who wasn't absolutely happy. Now and then he raised his head and sniffed the strange smells around him, but George didn't take any special notice of that. After all, she knew the thieves must be coming and going in the passage quite often, so of course he would pick up their scent.

When the children and Timmy arrived on the bank of the underground river, the children ran to the gang's old hiding places. Sure enough, the chests of stolen goods were back where they had been before!

'This is fantastic,' George exclaimed.

'Look!' said Dick. 'There's a little handcart here – the thieves must have used it to move their haul about the passages. Well, we can use it for *our* furniture removals too – getting the treasures back up to our bikes!'

He roared with laughter. And it was at that very moment that Julian noticed how oddly Timmy was behaving.

Timmy had stopped at the spot where the hidden passage began – the one leading to Riddington Hall. He was sniffing the air very hard, looking in the direction of the passage, with one forepaw raised.

'George – look at Timmy!' said Julian. 'He seems to be worried about something, doesn't he?'

'Oh, never mind him!' said George. She was helping Dick to put one of the chests into the little handcart. 'I expect he's picked up the scent of a rat or something! Here, come and lend a hand, Ju! This chest is terribly heavy. Mind your feet, Anne!'

Feeling rather uneasy, though he couldn't

quite have said why, Julian rejoined the others. With some difficulty, the four cousins got the chest in place on the little handcart. Suddenly, a loud bark from Tim made them all jump.

This time, now that their hard work was not absorbing all their attention, George, Dick and Anne turned their heads to look. Julian, who was already on his guard, jumped. He was very pale.

'The men!' he whispered. 'Quick – we'd better get out of here!'

But there was no time for the Five to escape. The three men they had thought were safely out of the way had just emerged from the passage joining the cave to Riddington Hall!

Eric, who was leading them, made straight for Julian. In a moment he had seized the boy and tied his hands together with a length of thin cord. Next, the big man grabbed Dick.

Meanwhile Manuel had thrown his jacket over Timmy's head to keep him quiet. Joe had his work cut out to overpower George! She hit and scratched and kicked like mad – but of course Joe was stronger than a young girl, however brave.

When at last, the Five found themselves powerless, Eric roared with laughter.

'Well, kiddies, so you thought you could run rings round us, the way we're running rings round the police? You certainly didn't know who you were dealing with! You may have managed to pinch our boat the other day, but you're in our

Eric, who was leading them, made straight for Julian.

'This is a rotten time for these kids to come interfering. I'm wondering what we'd better do with them.'

power now – you and that flea-bitten mongrel of yours!'

'Shut up, Eric!' said Joe, scowling. 'This is a rotten time for these kids to come interfering – just as we were going to make off with our haul! I'm wondering what we'd better do with them.' He gave George a furious look, and added, 'If I had *my* way I'd wring all their necks! That lad bit me like a wild thing – and that's what he is, too.'

This time, George didn't even notice that she'd been mistaken for a boy! She was seething with anger.

'I'm only sorry I didn't manage to bite you harder!' she said. 'But mark my words, the police will catch up with you sooner or later!'

'Oh, better gag the lot of 'em, Eric!' said Joe.

While the big man gagged the children, Manuel was saying, 'I can always dispose of the dog – shall I do it?'

George was shaking all over with terror, but Joe shook his head.

'No,' he said. 'Better avoid violence if we can. The trouble is, if we leave these kids here they could starve to death. And if they don't starve to death, and they're found – well, they won't waste any time before they start off after us again. You know, it may sound funny, but I feel they're almost as dangerous to us as the police! So the only thing we can do is take them along with us!'

Chapter Sixteen

A CAR JOURNEY BY NIGHT

Forcing their prisoners to go ahead of them, the gang of thieves set off along the underground passage, the way that the children had come. Manuel brought up the rear. He had stuffed poor Timmy into a sack which he was carrying over his shoulder. Timmy kicked frantically, trying to escape, but he couldn't – the sack was too tightly tied up, and he didn't have room to struggle very well.

George was still furious. Julian was horrified by the way their adventure had turned out, and Dick hadn't got over his surprise yet. Poor Anne was almost fainting with terror. Her knees felt as if they might give way any moment.

'I wonder where these ruffians are taking us?' thought George.

She was wondering, too, which way the criminals would choose to bring them all out into the open. If they had got hold of another boat somehow or other, they would most likely come out in the cave beside the sea. But if they were using a car or a van, they would go up to the cliff-top road. And that was just what happened. It was hard work even for a man as strong as Eric to haul the little handcart with the chests of treasures up the slope of the underground passage to the clump of gorse bushes.

Once they were at the end of the passage, the burglars hauled the children out into the open with them. The moonlight was very bright.

'This way!' was all Joe said.

They had to follow him towards a group of trees where there were two cars waiting in the shadows.

'A good thing we brought two cars, the way all this has turned out!' muttered Manuel.

'Well, you know Joe and his premonitions!' laughed Eric. 'He's very far-sighted, is Joe! Go on, you kids, get in!' he added, giving his prisoners a push.

Julian and Dick were pushed into one car with Eric at the wheel, while George and Anne found themselves on the back seat of the other with Joe driving. The two cars set off with Joe leading the way. It was not light enough for the children to be able to see the countryside around them, and after a few miles Anne fell asleep. She was quite exhausted with weariness and crying.

Manuel, who was sitting next to Joe, turned round from time to time.

'Hullo, the little girl's dropped off to sleep,' he said, seeing that Anne had closed her eyes. Like the other men, he thought Anne was the only girl in the party, and George was a boy!

His remark gave George an idea. After a while she let her own head nod, and pretended to be falling asleep herself. Soon afterwards Manuel turned round again.

'The boy's snoring too now,' he told his companion. 'And good riddance! That one's worse than all the other three put together!'

'I shan't feel happy till we've arrived and these kids are under lock and key,' said Joe.

He didn't seem to want to continue the conversation, so Manuel stopped talking.

As carefully as possible, taking advantage of every bump in the road, George wriggled her hands around until she had one of them free. Once she had done that, she got her handkerchief out of her pocket – that wasn't easy to do without being noticed. With even more difficulty, she started trying to work the square of white cotton through the car window, which was wound half-way down, until she could throw it out on to the road.

'If I can drop it out, it will at least be some sort of clue for anyone searching for us,' she thought. 'And when we've gone a little farther I'll throw out the identity bracelet Father gave me last

Christmas – and then my wallet.'

But unfortunately, Manuel didn't give George a chance to put her clever plan into action.

'You young schemer, you! Trying to leave a trail, eh? We're not having any of that, my lad!'

He had taken hold of George's wrist and was shaking her roughly. Frightened, Anne woke up with a start. Manuel watched the two girls like a hawk for the rest of the journey, and George felt angrier than ever.

At last the car ride ended, and the children were dragged out. They looked round. In the moonlight, they saw a long white building. There was no other house in sight anywhere near. Joe and his accomplices must have chosen this lonely place on purpose, so that no one would notice them coming and going.

Eric shoved the children forward.

'Hurry up and get inside! We've got no time to waste!'

He made them cross a kind of paved hall, and then ordered them to climb a staircase. On the first floor they saw another, very steep flight of steps leading to an attic, and Eric made the children climb this staircase too. Then, with Manuel's help, he took off their gags and untied them.

'Right – you can shout to your hearts' content in here, and no one will hear you!' he said. 'Sweet dreams!'

Manuel threw the sack with Timmy inside it down at George's feet. Then the two men disappeared, closing and locking the attic door after them. George quickly set poor Timmy free.

Julian had a quick look round the attic at once.

'There doesn't seem to be any way at all to get out,' he said gloomily. 'Well, we'd better try to get some sleep, and then we'll take stock of things tomorrow.'

Quite worn out, the Five lay down on the attic floor and closed their eyes.

Chapter Seventeen

THE ALARM IS RAISED

At home in Kirrin Cottage, Aunt Fanny and Uncle Quentin had no idea what risks the four children were running!

When they left in the evening, Aunt Fanny had a slight headache, so she went to bed early. Her husband, on the other hand, worked very late in the peace and quiet of his study on a very difficult experiment he was doing.

Before she went to sleep, Aunt Fanny told herself that the children were very sensible young people, and she was sure they wouldn't stay out too late. As for Uncle Quentin, he didn't even know that the Five had gone out at all!

So it was not until next morning that the scientist and his wife found the note George had left for them. Feeling surprised that the children had not come down for breakfast yet – and it was well past breakfast time! – Aunt Fanny went up to the room which Anne shared with George. She saw at once that the beds had not been slept in, and there was an envelope on one of the bedspreads, placed so that she would be sure to see it. She read the note inside.

'Oh, Quentin!' she called. Her voice was quite hoarse. 'Oh dear – this is terrible! Something dreadful must have happened to the children.'

Her husband ran upstairs and found her – she had collapsed into an armchair. She held out the note to him in a trembling hand. 'Read that, Quentin!'

Uncle Quentin did as she asked.

'They must be out of their minds!' he said angrily. 'Why on earth didn't they tell us? I'd have warned the police!'

'Oh, Quentin – quick! We must do something to help them!'

'Just keep calm, my dear. I'll see about it straight away.'

He ran downstairs like the wind, dashed into his study and picked up the telephone. A few moments later, all the police in the Kirrin area had been alerted.

It was quite a little army which set off to the cliff-top. Uncle Quentin, who was frantic with worry, kept urging the children's rescuers to make haste, and it was not long before they arrived. The weather was beautiful again today, and the sun was shining brightly in a blue sky, just as if no one could be in any kind of trouble.

Once they had reached the cliff-top, the police took all the correct precautions for going into the underground passages to capture the gang and rescue the children. Some of the men went down to the beach to block the entrance to the cave. A coastguard vessel had been alerted too, and it was already watching the mouth of the underground river. The rest of the policemen went down into the passage which came out in the middle of the gorse bushes.

Uncle Quentin insisted on going with the rescue party.

'My daughter and my niece and nephews are inside these caves!' he told the policemen. 'I really can't be expected to wait quietly outside to see what happens!'

The police inspector in charge of the rescuers had no alternative but to agree to let Uncle Quentin come with them.

'Very well, then,' he said. 'But be sure you don't make any noise. We must take these criminals by surprise – the children's safety is at stake.'

Unfortunately, however, careful as the policemen had been, it was no use. When they and Uncle Quentin finally came out on the banks of the underground river, they did not find anyone.

The whole gang had disappeared, taking the children with them! The police searched all the passages, exploring every nook and cranny of the underground network of caves, but they did not find anything – except the pretty ribbon Anne had worn to tie her hair back the day before, lying in one corner of the gang's cave.

Poor Uncle Quentin was in despair – and he had to go home and tell Aunt Fanny the bad news too.

Chapter Eighteen

PRISONERS IN THE ATTIC

Tired, worn-out and upset, the children slept surprisingly soundly on the hard boards of their prison floor until dawn.

Dick was the first to open his eyes. He looked round him, puzzled, not knowing where he was at first. Then his memory came back, and he shook the others awake.

'Come on, time to get up! Whatever we do, we *must* get out of here!'

Easier said than done!

'Let's have a really thorough look around,' suggested Julian. That didn't take long! When the four cousins inspected their attic prison they found that there were only two possible ways out – the door, which was locked, and very solid, and a skylight in the ceiling opening on to the slope of the roof.

'We're in a real mess now!' sighed Julian.

'What – what will they do to us?' stammered Anne. Her teeth were chattering with fright.

'Oh, Anne, for goodness' sake don't start weeping and wailing again!' said George. 'You know, I'm *furious* with myself for dragging you all into this adventure. It's my fault – I acted without thinking! I should have listened to Julian and been more careful.'

'You mustn't blame yourself,' Julian told her kindly. 'It was really up to me, as the eldest, to stop you, so it's quite as much my fault as yours! Here, Dick – give me a leg up, old fellow! I want to try looking out of that skylight. The window in it seems to open, and I think I can get up to it with some help from you. It's lucky the ceiling is quite low, because we haven't even got a table or chair in here to stand on!'

Dick gave his brother a leg up as Julian had asked, and Julian clung to the sill of the skylight with both hands and craned his neck to see out.

'Blow!' he said. 'All I can see is fields – and they're absolutely deserted!'

As they had no idea just where they were, the children settled down to try listening for any noises inside the house, in case they could pick up clues from that. George knelt on the floor and took Timmy by the scruff of his neck.

'Listen, Tim!' she told him. 'Listen!'

The dog obediently pricked up his ears, but that was all.

'Oh dear – I don't think there's anyone here at all!' sighed George. 'The house seems to be perfectly silent. The gang must have left.'

'Perhaps this isn't their real hideout?' said Anne in a low voice. 'Perhaps they just left us here on their way to somewhere else?'

'No, I should guess this is their den all right!'

'But why have they gone off, then?' asked Anne.

'They could be taking their loot abroad to dispose of it,' suggested Julian.

'Yes, you're probably right,' George agreed.

Suddenly Timmy growled, and the children froze.

'Someone's coming!' Dick whispered.

The steps of the attic staircase creaked as footsteps came up them, and the key turned in the lock. An unfriendly-looking woman appeared in the doorway.

'Here you are,' she said in a cross voice, putting a basket down on the floor. 'Food enough to last you till tomorrow.'

And she disappeared as abruptly as she had come, locking the door again behind her. George clenched her fists.

'Oh, how stupid we are!' she cried. 'We ought all to have jumped on her at once! There are five of us – we could have overpowered her!'

The dull sound of the front door closing echoed through the house. With Julian's help, Dick hoisted himself up to look out of the skylight this time.

'Yes, our jailer's just gone out,' he told the others. 'She's walking along the road towards a village – I can just see it in the distance.'

He slid to the ground again, scratching his head thoughtfully. 'What can we do?' he asked, baffled. 'This house seems to be empty, and here we are shut up in the attic!'

'We can only wait,' said Anne sadly. 'By now Uncle Quentin and Aunt Fanny must have found the note George left for them, and they'll go and tell the police.'

'Yes,' said Julian. 'And the police will go straight to the cave – and they won't find anyone there. A fat lot of good *that* will do us!'

'Why don't you stop talking and do something instead?' grumbled George. 'Obviously we've got to stand on our own feet – so first of all, we'd better get out of this attic.'

Her cousins stared at her as if they thought she was mad. 'But how?' they asked.

'Julian, you're good with your hands – and I've just noticed that that woman left the key in the lock. On the other side of the door, of course, but a little thing like that isn't going to stop you, is it?'

Julian let out a shout of glee.

'You're right, George, it certainly isn't! This won't be the first time I've retrieved a key with the help of – oh, but I haven't got a sheet of news-paper! Or a pencil either.'

'No,' said Dick, 'but look! Here's a flat piece of cardboard, and a bit of wire.'

He had just found both objects among the odds and ends of rubbish in one corner of the attic. Julian did not waste any time. He knelt down by the door and got to work. To start with, he slipped the cardboard under the door, making sure that he left enough of it on his side for him to be able to pull it back again. Then he worked the wire round in the keyhole until he had pushed the key out of the lock. It fell on the cardboard on the other side of the door. Now Julian should be able to pull the piece of cardboard back inside the attic, with the key on it!

Breathless with excitement, George, Dick, Anne – and even Timmy, who seemed to understand what was going on – gathered round him.

Gently, the boy pulled the cardboard towards him. It ought to have had the key on it – but the key must have been bigger than the children had expected, and, after all, it turned out to be too thick to slip through the gap between the bottom of the door and the floorboards themselves!

Julian stood up, looking rather pale and holding the useless piece of cardboard.

'Sorry,' he said. 'No good.'

There was a dismayed silence. Dick was the first to recover.

'Well, we're not done for yet!' he said, tapping his forehead. 'I've just had a brainwave – a brilliant, marvellous, amazing, fantastic idea, in fact, an idea worthy only of a genius like me!'

'Yes, yes, all right, you're a genius, Dick!' said George. 'But what's your idea exactly?'

'We escape over the rooftop! See?'

Julian and Anne did not reply, but George was enthusiastic.

'Wonderful!' she cried. 'You really *are* a genius after all, Dick! You're quite right, there's no other solution.'

'Here, take it easy!' said Julian. 'Do you want us all to break our necks, or what?'

'Certainly not!' said George. 'I have a very good head for heights, and I'm sure-footed too. So is Dick! You give him a leg up, Julian, and then *I'll* go up, and once we're out on the roof there must be some way we can get down to the ground. Then we'll come upstairs and let you and Anne out too.'

Dick and George insisted on trying to climb out, and Julian ended by giving in. As for Anne, she was so terrified and wanted to get away so badly that, just for once, she didn't object to the risks of Dick and George's daring plan!

Julian helped his brother and his cousin to haul themselves up through the window in the skylight and out on the roof. 'See you soon!' said George, before she disappeared.

Then she and Dick were making their way along the ridge of the roof, bent low and going almost on all fours. They took great care not to slip. One badly judged movement, and they would tumble off into space.

'George,' whispered Dick, after a few moments, 'how do you think we can get down?'

'Come on – oh, go carefully along this sloping bit! There should be a drainpipe somewhere over here!'

George was right, but it was dangerous climbing down it. If the two cousins lost their grip, it was more than likely they might break an arm or leg as they fell to the ground.

'Well, too bad!' said George under her breath. 'Whatever happens, we *must* get down!'

It took all the strength, skill and courage George and Dick could summon up to manage the risky climb down. Clinging to the drainpipe which ran to the ground from the guttering along the edge of the roof, they tried to get a series of good grips with their hands and feet, but every now and then their fingers or heels slipped, and they only just stopped themselves falling. Luckily they kept their heads the whole time.

And at last they were safe on the ground! George felt very proud of their success. Julian would have been a little too heavy and Anne quite a lot too frightened to manage the climb down as she and Dick had done! As for Timmy, the poor

They took great care not to slip. One badly judged movement, and they would tumble off into space.

Every now and then their fingers or heels slipped.

dog could never have followed his little mistress down the drainpipe.

'And now to find a way to get back into the house, Dick!' she said.

That was easier than they might have expected. The doors and windows were tightly closed and locked, but there was a trapdoor into the coal cellar, which was not fastened properly. Thanks to this oversight, Dick and George were able to get into the basement of the house quite easily – and they didn't even get dirty, because it was a long time since anyone had kept coal in the coal cellar! Skirting the central heating boiler which stood in the middle of the cellar, the two cousins found a small flight of steps leading up to a door.

'I only hope this door isn't bolted on the other side,' said George, suddenly feeling worried.

But luckily her fears were needless. The door was only closed with a simple latch. Dick lifted the latch, and the two children found themselves in a huge kitchen with flagstones on the floor. The kitchen opened straight into the front hall.

They grinned at each other. They had done it!

Chapter Nineteen

HITCHING A LIFT

After that, George and Dick didn't waste any time. They made for the stairs and ran up them four steps at once.

When they reached the attic door, Dick picked up the key from where it had fallen on the floor, and let Julian, Anne and Timmy out.

Anne was crying with relief, Tim was barking, and Julian clapped his brother and his cousin on the shoulder.

'Well done indeed!' he said. 'Congratulations! Now, we must hurry! Let's explore the house before we escape. But we must be quick.'

It had to be a rapid inspection of the place, because they knew they didn't have much time. It seemed to be a big farmhouse – a very modern one. No doubt Joe, Eric and Manuel had chosen it because it was so isolated, and they were planning to lie low here and wait for a chance to get out of the country.

'We saw them bring their loot out of the cave – if it's here, it must be well hidden somewhere,' said Julian thoughtfully. 'They wouldn't want to lug those chests with them everywhere they went.'

The rooms on the first floor and ground floor did not reveal anything odd. The young friends searched them, but they saw nothing suspicious. However, down in the basement a room next to the coal cellar did look promising. Its huge door was fitted with no less than three enormous brand new locks. The steel of the locks shone brightly in the dim light.

'Hm,' said George. 'Those locks look as if they were put on quite recently – and why would they be there except to lock up some kind of treasure?'

'You're right,' said Julian. 'I bet the stolen property is hidden in there for the time being, until the gang can get it out of the country!'

'Oh, do let's be quick and go and tell the police!' whispered Anne, who hated hanging around in such a dangerous place.

They went back to the coal cellar, climbed out through the trapdoor, and found themselves out in the open.

'Whew! Free at last!' said Julian happily. 'I say, it's really good to get your lungs full of fresh country air again!'

'Oh, Ju, don't stand there talking about fresh air!' Anne begged him. 'Let's hurry! I can't wait to get well away from here. Just suppose the gang come back – or that woman!'

'Don't worry, Anne,' said Dick. 'The provisions she brought us were supposed to last till tomorrow, or so she said. That must mean she won't be back before then!'

'I'm not so sure of that,' said George. She was already setting off along the road. 'She went off on foot, didn't she? So she probably hasn't gone far. In any case, I think we should keep our eyes well open. If we see anyone suspicious coming towards us, we must get off the road and hide. I don't want to be locked up again, thank you very much!'

The children walked on in silence. They did not recognise the countryside round them at all. They were going along a minor road, and it seemed to stretch on for ever and ever. They could only just make out a church tower in the distance, to show them that the village Dick had seen from the sky-light lay in that direction.

The sun was quite high in the sky now. The children were perspiring, and Timmy was panting.

'At this rate, we'll be exhausted before we get to the village!' said George. 'Why don't we hitch a lift?'

'Too risky,' Julian told her. 'Just suppose we

stopped one of the thieves' cars! Anyway, there isn't a car in sight!'

As if to contradict him, they suddenly heard the sound of a car's engine.

The Five turned to look. Yes – a long, low sports car was coming in their direction. They were sure it was not a bit like the cars the thieves had been driving.

George didn't hesitate for a moment. She stood right in the middle of the road and waved her arms. The sports car came up to her, braked and stopped. There was a young man at the wheel.

'Hullo there, kids!' he said cheerfully. 'What's up? Missed your bus?'

'No, sir,' said Julian politely, stepping forward. 'Something much more serious. Could you possibly give us a lift to the nearest village? We must go to a police station.'

'A police station?' said the driver in surprise. 'All right! So long as you're not running away from home, or anything like that!'

On the way, the children quickly explained what it was all about. Their new friend was very interested, and he went to the police station with them to tell the police just where he had met them, so as to back up their statement.

The quiet little country police station had never known such excitement before!

Of course Uncle Quentin and the Kirrin police had made sure that a nation-wide alert had gone out for the missing children, so the policemen here knew all about the Five and the gang of thieves. The first thing they did was to telephone Kirrin police station, so that George's parents could have their minds set at rest as soon as possible.

Then, after sending for some reinforcements to come quickly, they organised an expedition to go and trap the gang.

'We shall need you to come along and show us just where the farmhouse is, so that we can surround it,' the inspector in charge of the party of policemen told the children. Of course, they were delighted to help.

Soon they were all ready to leave. Patrick Bartlett, the young man with the sports car who had been so helpful to the Five, asked if he could join the expedition too.

'And if you like,' he suggested to the inspector, 'I could give these young people a lift in my car again. That would leave you more room for your own men.'

The inspector was happy to accept this kind offer. 'Thank you very much, sir!' he said.

George and her cousins couldn't have asked for anything better than another ride in their new friend's beautiful car. Timmy curled up as small as he could at George's feet. He had made it very clear that he had no intention of staying behind! So the white sports car started off, with three police cars following it. It was very important for them to reach the farm before the gang and their woman accomplice got back, so as to set a police trap for them.

Chapter Twenty

SIR DONALD TO THE RESCUE!

Everything went smoothly. The children showed the policemen the house where they had been kept prisoner, and the inspector and two of his men made sure that no one had returned there since the children left. Then he gave orders for the police cars to be hidden behind a big farm building. Finally, he stationed half of his men outside the house, hidden in the shelter of trees and bushes.

'And now for us!' he told the children. 'We'd better get inside quickly. I sent an expert to pick the lock of the front door as soon as we arrived. You young people are to go up to the first floor with Mr Bartlett here – you'll be quite safe there. The rest of us will set the trap for those villains indoors. So come along! We'll close the front door behind us, so that it will look as if nothing's wrong.'

Soon the Five and Patrick, up on the first-floor landing, were peering with interest through the bars of the banisters. None of the people inside the house moved.

'There are policemen posted all round the hall, ready to jump out when the gang come through the door!' Julian whispered.

'*I* think this is silly!' Anne whispered back. 'I mean, Eric and the others may easily not come back here till tomorrow – or even later!'

'Yes, but that woman will be back before then!' said George. 'She left the house on foot, remember, and without any luggage. So as I said before, she can't have gone very far. The police will be counting on that.'

'Sssh!' said Patrick quietly. 'Listen!'

Down below, the silence in the hall had just been broken by one of the policemen. 'Watch out, sir!' he said to the inspector, in a low voice. 'I can see a woman coming along the road. Yes – she's coming this way sure enough!'

The inspector hurried to join the policeman, who was on watch with a pair of binoculars at a window beside the front door. He passed the binoculars to the inspector.

'See for yourself, sir!'

The inspector raised the binoculars and looked out of the window. He smiled. Then he beckoned to George, who ran downstairs.

'Here!' he told her. 'You have a look, Miss Kirrin, and tell me if you recognise her.'

'Yes!' said George. 'Oh, yes – that's the woman

who was acting as our jailer!'

'Right – you nip back upstairs to the others, then, and whatever you do, keep quiet and don't move. She'll be here in a minute or so.'

George did as the inspector said, and the Five waited, pressed close together, their hearts beating fast, to see what would happen next.

Feeling rather worried, Anne squeezed her big brother's arm. 'Julian, I'm frightened!' she whispered.

'Sssh, Anne! Keep quiet!'

'What's going to happen?'

'The police will arrest that woman, that's all. She's an accomplice of the gang who burgled all those stately homes, so she jolly well deserves what she gets!'

Up on the landing, the children stopped whispering, and down below in the hall the police stood absolutely still and quiet, ready to spring.

In the silence, they heard footsteps approaching outside. A key was turned in the lock, and from where they were standing the children saw the door open. Golden sunlight flooded in on the paved floor.

Not suspecting anything, the woman who had visited the Five in their attic prison came in.

Then everything happened very fast. Two policemen emerged from the shadows in the hall, took hold of the woman's arms and overpowered her, although she struggled with them.

'Who are you? What do you want?' she shouted.

'I'd have thought you could tell who we are from our uniforms, ma'am,' said one of the policemen. 'As for what we want – we want to know who *you* are!'

'I'm not saying anything!' yelped the woman furiously. 'Not a word! You have no right to do this!'

'Oh, so you don't think we have any right to do it?' said the inspector, coming out of hiding and walking up to her. 'Be careful what you say, ma'am! I should warn you that it may be taken down and used in evidence against you. I'm arresting you for aiding and abetting the gang that burgled Riddington Hall and a number of other stately homes in the neighbourhood of Kirrin. For all I know, you may be an active member of the gang yourself.'

'I don't know what you're talking about!' cried the woman. 'I deny everything!'

'Including keeping these children prisoners in your attic?' asked the inspector, pointing to the Five on the first-floor landing.

The woman looked up and glared at the children, full of hatred. Then she said, shrugging her shoulders, 'I don't even know who they are!'

'Witnesses for the prosecution, ma'am – that's who they are!'

At that moment they all heard a car's engine in the distance. The policeman with the binoculars, who had taken up his post at the window again, told the inspector, 'There's a car coming now, sir, with three men in it. One tall fair man, and a couple of smaller dark men, one of them with a beard.'

'That's them!' cried George. 'Those are the men who kidnapped us!'

'We'll be asking you and your cousins to identify them officially in a minute, Miss Kirrin. Just stay up there a little longer! As for you, ma'am – not a word out of you to warn your accomplices, or you'll be sorry!'

Down in the hall, the inspector drew the woman into the background. There was silence again, and the children and Patrick waited with bated breath. The showdown was coming any moment now! Would everything work out the way they hoped?

They heard the car stop quite close to the house, and then Eric's loud voice.

'Hullo there, Miriam!' he called. 'Are you in? We've got news! We shall be off tomorrow!'

As he spoke, Eric pushed the door open – and the woman called Miriam suddenly wrenched herself free of the inspector and shouted, 'Watch out, Eric! Run for it! The police are on to us!'

There was a moment's silence, and then the men could be heard running away from the front door. The inspector, looking furious, raised a whistle to his lips. He blew it – the sound was intended to give warning to the policemen stationed outside the house. But by the time they had come round to the front door the gang could easily have made their getaway, so the inspector and the men inside the house gave chase themselves.

The Five and Patrick were already on their way downstairs, and they ran out of the doorway too.

They stopped dead for a moment at the sight before them! The three criminals were running towards their car, parked among the trees a little way off. And George immediately realised that they were going to escape their pursuers – the police cars were still round at the other side of the house, hidden by the farm building.

She did not hesitate for a moment.

'Go on, Timmy – get them! Good dog! *Bite* them, Tim!'

Timmy didn't wait to be told twice. In three bounds, he was after the men.

Eric heard him coming and turned round, raising an arm to defend himself – just in time to protect his throat. Timmy's jaws had been about to close on it!

'Clear off – get away, will you!' yelled Eric, making faces and trying to get his arm away from the dog. Timmy was holding it in a firm and painful grip. And Timmy was not going to let him go! In a moment the police arrived.

As soon as they had arrested Eric and taken

'Clear off - get away, will you!' yelled Eric.

Joe struggled out, half stunned, and still struggling with brave old Timmy.

him into custody, Timmy lost interest in the man, and raced off after the other two criminals. He had a particular grudge against Manuel, for tying him up in that sack!

When Manuel turned round to see the dog's threatening jaws and gleaming eyes so close to him, he felt so terrified that Timmy had no trouble at all in overpowering him. As the dog jumped at him, Manuel fainted with terror and fell flat on the ground.

That meant there was only Joe left. Joe had actually reached the car – he wasn't stopping to bother about his companions. He jumped into the driving seat. The engine was still warm. It started at once, and the car moved away.

The policemen gave exclamations of annoyance. Patrick, Julian, Dick and Anne were watching in dismay – but George wasn't beaten yet!

'Go on, Timmy, get him!' she shouted to her dog.

Timmy had almost reached the car when it drove past him, and he might have given up the attempt but for that last shout from his little mistress. Her voice spurred him on to make a final effort!

Suddenly he gathered speed, and with one powerful spring he leaped right into the car. It was not going very fast yet, and Joe had been in such a hurry to start off that he had not closed the door. He had to let go of the steering wheel to defend himself from the dog. Then everything seemed to happen all at once. Out of control, the car crashed into a tree! Joe staggered out, half stunned, and still struggling with brave old Timmy. The inspector and his men arrived on the scene, rather breathless, and now all they had to do was arrest Joe, the gang-leader. He didn't seem to be in very good shape when Timmy left the police to deal with him!

A few moments later, the inspector was looking at Eric, Joe, Manuel and Miriam with satisfaction. They cut a sorry figure in handcuffs!

'Well now,' he said, after congratulating George warmly and patting Timmy, 'well now, my young friends, I'm going to take you back to the village. I should think your father will have arrived to collect you by now, Georgina. But first we'll just have a little look at this den of thieves!'

The children had been quite right. The three stout locks on the cellar door didn't stand up to the policemen for long, and when they had broken down the door and explored the room beyond it, they found all the valuables stolen from the stately homes near Kirrin by Joe and his gang.

'And here are Sir Donald's gold watches, too!' said George happily. 'How pleased he'll be to get them back!'

A little later, after saying goodbye to Patrick Bartlett, the Five and the police – and their prisoners too, of course – got back to the village and the police station. Uncle Quentin, who had just arrived, looked very angry when he saw the children.

'Well, if you're expecting praise from *me*, you're in for a disappointment!' he said. 'Your mother was quite ill with worry over your escapade, Georgina. As for you, Julian – you're the eldest, I should have expected you to show a little more sense! I shall find it very hard to forgive you for the fright you gave your poor Aunt Fanny.'

The children looked very upset – and it was no good for the inspector, who was surprised to find that Uncle Quentin could be so stern, to try calming him down. Uncle Quentin refused to listen.

'You will be punished,' he told the children as he drove them home to Kirrin Cottage in his car. 'To begin with, I'm confiscating your new bicycles – the Kirrin police brought them home. As for Timothy, he'll have to stay chained up in his kennel until the end of the holidays. And it's no good trying to argue with me!'

By the time two days had passed, George and her cousins were beginning to think they'd never spent such miserable holidays before! They were kicking their heels at Kirrin Cottage, without being able to go out for expeditions on their bikes. They were so bored they didn't even have the heart to play games. George absolutely refused to leave Timmy's side, and Julian, Dick and

Anne kept her company by his kennel.

'It just isn't fair!' sighed Dick. 'It's all thanks to us that the gang's behind bars, and the stately homes have their treasures back – Sir Donald Riddington's got his gold watches back too!'

'Speaking of Sir Donald,' said Anne, looking at the front gate, 'here he is at this very moment!'

And it *was* Sir Donald, looking happy and cheerful and ten years younger! He had heard, from the inspector who arrested the gang, that his 'young heroes', as he called them, were in trouble, and so he had come to try and pay his debt of gratitude.

How did he manage to soften Uncle Quentin's heart and persuade him to let the children off their punishments? Well, no one knew for certain! But after talking to George's parents, he appeared out in the garden again, smiling broadly and carrying the key of the shed where Uncle Quentin had locked up the new bikes.

He showed it to the children. 'There – now you can take that dog off his chain, and off you all go for a nice ride!' he said.

They were delighted! George jumped up and kissed him. 'Thank you – oh, thank you!' she cried happily.

'Well, well, my dear,' he said, smiling, 'it seems to me that if anyone should be saying "thank you", it's me! So I *will* say "thank you", with all my heart, my dear young friends. And thank *you*, too,

Timmy – what a fine dog you are!'

And very gravely, Sir Donald shook paws with Timmy.

If you have enjoyed this book here are some
more that you might like to read, also
published by Knight Books:

THE FAMOUS FIVE AND THE
MYSTERY OF THE EMERALDS

A new adventure of the characters created by
Enid Blyton. Told by Claude Voilier, translated
by Anthea Bell

A summer holiday camping on Kirrin Island is the
prospect in store for the Five, and they're
eagerly looking forward to exploring the
island.
But when George overhears a couple of crooks
planning a jewel robbery, the Famous Five set
off on a dangerous and thrilling trail.

KNIGHT BOOKS

A complete list of the FAMOUS FIVE
ADVENTURES by Enid Blyton:

All of these titles are also available in a
hard-cover edition published by Hodder and
Stoughton Children's Books

KNIGHT BOOKS

STARSTORMERS
SUNBURST

NICHOLAS FISK

Four children have escaped a tired, depleted
Earth in a homemade spaceship. It is a desperate
attempt to find their parents, who are
working to establish a new settlement on a
distant planet.
These first two exciting titles in the
Starstormer saga follow their nerve-racking
adventures, alone in space, and their fight
against the evil forces of the Octopus Emperor.

Coming soon . . . CATFANG, the third in the
series.

KNIGHT BOOKS

☐ 26524 8   THE FAMOUS FIVE AND
                  THE MYSTERY OF THE
                  EMERALDS   75p
☐ 24878 5   STARSTORMERS   85p
☐ 24879 3   SUNBURST   85p

All these books are available at your local bookshop or newsagent, or can be ordered direct from the publisher. Just tick the titles you want and fill in the form below.

Prices and availability subject to change without notice.

KNIGHT BOOKS—P.O. Box 11, Falmouth, Cornwall.

Please send cheque or postal order, and allow the following for postage and packing.

U.K.—One book 30p, 15p for the second book plus 12p each for additional book ordered, up to a maximum of £1.29.

B.F.P.O. and EIRE—30p for the first book, 15p for the second book plus 12p per copy for the next 7 books; thereafter 6p per book.

OTHER OVERSEAS CUSTOMERS—50p for the first book plus 15p per copy for each additional book.

Name ....

Address ....

....